W9-CYY-853

SOCIAL ISSUES
FIRSTHAND

| Depression

Other Books in the Social Issues Firsthand Series:

SOCIAL ISSUES
FIRSTHAND

Depression

Laurie Willis, Book Editor

GREENHAVEN PRESS

An imprint of Thomson Gale, a part of The Thomson Corporation

THOMSON

™

GALE

Detroit • New York • San Francisco • New Haven, Conn. • Waterville, Maine • London

07-2474

Christine Nasso, *Publisher*
Elizabeth Des Chenes, *Managing Editor*

© 2008 The Gale Group.

Star logo is a trademark and Gale and Greenhaven Press are registered trademarks used herein under license.

For more information, contact:
Greenhaven Press
27500 Drake Rd.
Farmington Hills, MI 48331-3535
Or you can visit our Internet site at http://www.gale.com

Articles in Greenhaven Press anthologies are often edited for length to meet page requirements. In addition, original titles of these works are changed to clearly present the main thesis and to explicitly indicate the author's opinion. Every effort is made to ensure that Greenhaven Press accurately reflects the original intent of the authors. Every effort has been made to trace the owners of copyrighted material.

Cover photograph reproduced by permission of © Anthony Redpath/Corbis.

LIBRARY OF CONGRESS CATALOGING-IN-PUBLICATION DATA

Depression / Laurie Willis, book editor.
   p. cm. -- (Social issues firsthand)
   Includes bibliographical references and index.
   ISBN-13: 978-0-7377-3836-0 (hardcover)
   1. Depression, Mental--Juvenile literature. 2. Depression in adolescence--Juvenile literature. I. Willis, Laurie.
   RC537.D4262 2008
   616.85'27--dc22
                                     2007028825

ISBN-10: 0-7377-3836-7 (hardcover)

Contents

Chapter 3: Getting Help

Chapter 4: How Depression Affects Others

Foreword

Social issues are often viewed in abstract terms. Pressing challenges such as poverty, homelessness, and addiction are viewed as problems to be defined and solved. Politicians, social scientists, and other experts engage in debates about the extent of the problems, their causes, and how best to remedy them. Often overlooked in these discussions is the human dimension of the issue. Behind every policy debate over poverty, homelessness, and substance abuse, for example, are real people struggling to make ends meet, to survive life on the streets, and to overcome addiction to drugs and alcohol. Their stories are ubiquitous and compelling. They are the stories of everyday people—perhaps your own family members or friends—and yet they rarely influence the debates taking place in state capitols, the national Congress, or the courts.

The disparity between the public debate and private experience of social issues is well illustrated by looking at the topic of poverty. Each year the U.S. Census Bureau establishes a poverty threshold. A household with an income below the threshold is defined as poor, while a household with an income above the threshold is considered able to live on a basic subsistence level. For example, in 2003 a family of two was considered poor if its income was less than $12,015; a family of four was defined as poor if its income was less than $18,810. Based on this system, the bureau estimates that 35.9 million Americans (12.5 percent of the population) lived below the poverty line in 2003, including 12.9 million children below the age of eighteen.

Commentators disagree about what these statistics mean. Social activists insist that the huge number of officially poor Americans translates into human suffering. Even many families that have incomes above the threshold, they maintain, are likely to be struggling to get by. Other commentators insist

9

that the statistics exaggerate the problem of poverty in the United States. Compared to people in developing countries, they point out, most so-called poor families have a high quality of life. As stated by journalist Fidelis Iyebote, "Cars are owned by 70 percent of 'poor' households. . . . Color televisions belong to 97 percent of the 'poor' [and] videocassette recorders belong to nearly 75 percent. . . . Sixty-four percent have microwave ovens, half own a stereo system, and over a quarter possess an automatic dishwasher."

However, this debate over the poverty threshold and what it means is likely irrelevant to a person living in poverty. Simply put, poor people do not need the government to tell them whether they are poor. They can see it in the stack of bills they cannot pay. They are aware of it when they are forced to choose between paying rent or buying food for their children. They become painfully conscious of it when they lose their homes and are forced to live in their cars or on the streets. Indeed, the written stories of poor people define the meaning of poverty more vividly than a government bureaucracy could ever hope to. Narratives composed by the poor describe losing jobs due to injury or mental illness, depict horrific tales of childhood abuse and spousal violence, recount the loss of friends and family members. They evoke the slipping away of social supports and government assistance, the descent into substance abuse and addiction, the harsh realities of life on the streets. These are the perspectives on poverty that are too often omitted from discussions over the extent of the problem and how to solve it.

Greenhaven Press's Social Issues Firsthand series provides a forum for the often-overlooked human perspectives on society's most divisive topics of debate. Each volume focuses on one social issue and presents a collection of ten to sixteen narratives by those who have had personal involvement with the topic. Extra care has been taken to include a diverse range of perspectives. For example, in the volume on adoption, readers will find the stories of birth parents who have made an adoption plan, adoptive parents, and adoptees themselves. After exposure to these varied points of view, the reader will have a clearer understanding that adoption is an intense, emotional experience full of joyous highs and painful lows for all concerned.

The debate surrounding embryonic stem cell research illustrates the moral and ethical pressure that the public brings to bear on the scientific community. However, while nonexperts often criticize scientists for not considering the potential negative impact of their work, ironically the public's reaction against such discoveries can produce harmful results as well. For example, although the outcry against embryonic stem cell research in the United States has resulted in fewer embryos being destroyed, those with Parkinson's, such as actor Michael J. Fox, have argued that prohibiting the development of new stem cell lines ultimately will prevent a timely cure for the disease that is killing Fox and thousands of others.

Each book in the series contains several features that enhance its usefulness, including an in-depth introduction, an annotated table of contents, bibliographies for further research, a list of organizations to contact, and a thorough index. These elements—combined with the poignant voices of people touched by tragedy and triumph—make the Social Issues Firsthand series a valuable resource for research on today's topics of political discussion.

Introduction

Clinical depression is one of the most common mental illnesses. The National Institute of Mental Health reported in 2005 that depression affects almost 20 million Americans each year. People suffering from depression experience feelings of sadness, despair, emptiness, or loss of interest or pleasure in nearly all things. Even though depression is a treatable illness with complete or partial success in most cases, many cases of depression are never treated, and others go untreated for years.

Beliefs and Misconceptions

There are a variety of reasons why depression goes untreated. Quite a few involve beliefs and misconceptions about this illness. People often feel there is a stigma attached to depression. They feel ashamed and embarrassed to admit to being depressed. Some consider depression to be a personality flaw, believing that depressed people are just lazy and should be able to "snap out of it." Depressed people believe this too, thinking that they can handle depression on their own.

Certain cultures, for example Latinos and African Americans, that place a particularly high value on self-reliance, see seeking help for depression as a sign of weakness. This can also be true of other groups, including older adults and people living in rural communities. In small, rural communities confidentiality is a problem, too, and it is difficult to receive treatment without being observed by friends and neighbors.

Assuming That Feelings of Depression Are Normal

Many people, particularly women, assume that depression is just a part of getting older. According to a 1996 survey by the National Mental Health Association, more than one-half of women believe it is "normal" for a woman to be depressed during menopause and that treatment is not necessary, and more than one-half of women believe depression is a "normal part of aging."

Symptoms of depression are usually episodic; that is, they come and go intermittently with periods of normalcy in between. This pattern reinforces the belief that depression can be handled without treatment. It disappears for periods of time and seems to have been conquered, only to appear again at another time.

Taking Drugs or Avoiding Them

At times, people choose to self-medicate, using alcohol or nonprescribed drugs to mask their depression. Others fear that drugs, even medications prescribed by a doctor, might be addictive so they don't want to get treatment. They may also fear feeling artificially happy all the time. In a 2006 survey by *Men's Health* magazine, only 40 percent of the men surveyed said they would take antidepressants if they were prescribed by their doctor, while 60 percent said they would choose to deal with the problem on their own.

The Influence of Physicians, Employers, and Insurance Companies

Medical professionals often overlook symptoms of depression when a patient also has other physical symptoms. According to a 1999 study reported in the *New England Journal of Medicine*, nearly 70 percent of depressed patients sought treatment for physical symptoms. Another study, conducted by Dr. Irene Mangani and presented at a meeting of the Gerontological Society of America, compared patient's scores on the Geriatric Depression Scale to the prevalence of symptoms identified by their primary care physicians; the doctors missed a significant number of symptoms indicating depression.

Sometimes there are practical reasons why people do not seek treatment for depression. People often fear repercussions by their employer. A University of Michigan Depression Center survey published in *Managed Care Weekly* in 2004 reports that 41 percent of workers surveyed felt that people could not acknowledge having depression at their workplace without jeopardizing their careers. On the other hand, benefit managers who were surveyed believe this is not true. Eighty-six percent of benefit managers surveyed said that reporting depression would not affect an employee's career. But unless employees are convinced it is safe to do so, they will continue to avoid seeking treatment, fearing their employer will find out.

Medical insurance can be an issue, too. Insurance may force a person to be treated by a primary care provider when a mental health specialist would be more appropriate. According to a 1994 article in the *Archives of Family Medicine*, some physicians deliberately substitute an alternate diagnosis instead of depression so that insurance reimbursement will not be a problem.

Public Opinion Is Changing

Public opinion about depression is changing. A survey by the National Mental Health Association in 2001 found that 55 percent of Americans polled believed that depression is a disease. In a similar survey ten years before, this figure was only 38 percent. The same survey reported that 48 percent of those surveyed had at least one friend or family member who suffers from depression.

As general beliefs about depression change, and as people who suffer from depression tell their stories, the number of people willing to seek treatment should increase. Some of the stigma should begin to fall away and depression can be handled like any other medical condition.

This book examines the disease through personal accounts that explore various aspects of depression, including what it's like to live with depression, the rewards and challenges of receiving treatment, and the experiences of family and friends dealing with the depression of a loved one.

SOCIAL ISSUES
FIRSTHAND

CHAPTER 1

Depression Strikes

Keeping Depression a Secret

Anna-Lisa Johanson

Anna-Lisa Johanson came from a family where depression and suicide were prevalent. Her grandfather committed suicide, as did two of her uncles. Her mother had suffered from mental illness since before Johanson was born, and the family expected Johanson to follow in her mother's footsteps, which she did.

After her mother killed herself by kneeling in front of an oncoming train, Johanson tried to publicly cover up her mother's mental illness, in the same way that she had spent many years keeping her own bipolar disorder a secret from those around her. Eventually, she met a role model who was brave enough to speak publicly about his mental illness. Johanson's outlook changed; she decided to speak out about herself and to study to become an advocate for the mentally ill.

My nine-month-old daughter is the most beautiful and perfect creature in the world. I stare at her every day with awe and love. When she nurses, she clutches my hand and looks deep into my soul, and I can hardly believe that I once thought I would never have children.

My genes and family history seemed too terrible to pass on to a new life. I grew up knowing that two of my uncles had committed suicide; I later learned that my grandfather committed suicide as well. By the time I was born, my mother had been suffering from mental illness for several years, and even as a small child, I knew she was sick. My father did everything he could to hold our family together, but my mother's illness tore us apart. When my parents finally divorced, he got custody of me and my three siblings.

I looked just like my mother: I had her smile, her hair, and some of her expressions. All through my childhood, I felt watched, as if family and friends were waiting for me to show symptoms of the illness that took her away from them. I'm lucky they were so vigilant. Like my mother, I suffer from a bipolar disorder and have been on medication, off and on, since I was 14.

My mother, I was told, got sicker each time she gave birth. She would be healthy and happy while pregnant, but during the postpartum period, her mood swings would become increasingly dramatic. Eventually I concluded that being pregnant would make me go crazy too.

Mother's Suicide

When my mother committed suicide in 1998 by kneeling in front of an oncoming train, only a handful of people knew about my illness. I did everything I could to keep my secret. It wasn't easy: My mother's disease played out in the public eye—she became famous as David Letterman's stalker.

Following her death, it took less than 24 hours for my name to appear in the papers. The walls around my life—I had recently gotten married and was two months into my first year of law school—came crashing down. I returned to class with a feeling of fear and dread. I thought people would judge me harshly and start watching to see if I, too, was sick.

At the time of my mother's death, I gave a few interviews to set the record straight. I wanted to say how beautiful she was, and that she died of a terrible disease that was nothing to be ashamed of. I wanted to share memories of my mother from before the illness completely took over her life. She was warm, intelligent, and loving. I know she did a good job of nurturing me as an infant and toddler or I would not have grown into the person I am. I wanted the world to know that my mother was not just the crazy woman in the papers.

But I only wanted to redeem the image of my mother—I still needed to keep my own secret. If I was meant to use my mother's death as a vehicle to come to terms with my own illness, I failed miserably. Asked point-blank on national television whether I was afraid of getting her disease, I unflinchingly said that I was past the usual age of onset.

Reasons for Secrecy

Over the years, I'd had many experiences that shaped my need for secrecy. When I was in elementary and middle school, my flamboyantly dressed mother would show up at recess, unannounced, just wanting to see me and hang out. I would go to her because I loved her and felt protective of her. But later, the other children would taunt me. Any time that someone wanted to pick a fight, all they had to do was say that my mom was crazy, and I would fly into a rage. I ended up being a bit of a bully and suspicious of other kids.

Early in college, I got involved in an intense, romantic relationship, and after a year, I decided to tell the man I was seeing that I suffered from a bipolar disorder. Our relationship meant the world to me. It was the first time I had fallen in love, and he was the first person who made me feel pretty just by the way he looked at me. We planned a romantic weekend escape to a cabin in the mountains, where I would make my revelation.

At the time, I was taking five different drugs: sleeping pills and an antianxiety medication before bedtime, and a combination of a mood stabilizer and two antidepressants to get through the day. When we got to the cabin, I left my little pharmacy out on the nightstand for him to see. In retrospect, I would not recommend this method of coming out.

At the end of the weekend, this man told me he was not the kind of person I needed in my life. He said I needed someone very strong—and that he couldn't be that someone. What I heard was, "You are too broken and not worth the hassle." It was the last time I let a man get close to me until I met my wonderful husband, who is loving and supportive and knows my moods slightly better than I do.

Other experiences in college reinforced my belief that I must, at all costs, keep my illness to myself. When I went to the student health center to be treated for a minor problem— headaches or stomach pains—the doctor on call would stop reading my chart as soon as he saw I was undergoing treatment for bipolar disorder. I had to persuade him that my symptoms were not side effects of my medication or manifestations of mental illness. If trained physicians had such a reaction, I thought, it was a pretty safe bet that other people would too.

Support from a Fellow Sufferer

But the most compelling reason not to go public was my fear that I would never be able to practice law. I had wanted to be a lawyer ever since I had negotiated bedtimes as a toddler. My plan included going straight to law school from college and becoming a class-action litigator. I believed that if the truth came out, I wouldn't be allowed to take the bar, let alone be hired by a good firm.

In the summer of 2000, I went to work as an intern for the Treatment Advocacy Center, a nonprofit group in Arlington, Virginia, that helps the mentally ill. (I now work there part-time as a legal assistant.) I learned that the assistant director, an attorney named Jonathan Stanley, also suffered from a bipolar disorder and had suffered a serious episode in college for which he was hospitalized. It took me a few weeks before I felt comfortable enough to ask Jon about his experience becoming a lawyer. He told me that after passing the bar, he had to go through three sets of interviews before different review panels in order to get a license to practice.

His bravery and outspokenness helped persuade me to start telling others about my illness. Partly because of my work with him and with the center, my life goals also changed. I'm now pursuing a joint degree in law, from Georgetown University, and public health, from Johns Hopkins, so that I can become a full-time advocate for the mentally ill. Maybe I can help other young women not to feel as utterly alone as I once did.

Getting Help and Speaking Out

Each time my mother got sick—and did not seek treatment— her condition would deteriorate. After 20 years of not being treated, she reached the point where she could never go back to the way she was before. Although I have a similar disorder, I was able to get help early on. And I've been told there is no reason to believe I will ever get any worse than I am now.

I've had only one truly manic episode—in college, when I was taking six classes and holding down three jobs to pay for school. At the end of the semester, I stayed up for three days straight, studying for final exams and writing research papers. At the time I thought I was brilliant and could take on the world—and indeed, this great manic episode propelled me onto the dean's list. But after sleeping for a few days, I fell into a depression and had to seek medical help.

The form of mental illness I have is called bipolar II, which means I am more likely to suffer from depression than from mania, its frenzied opposite. When I am getting depressed, I often don't recognize what's happening, until one morning I can't get out of bed and I feel like I hate the world. That's when I call my psychiatrist (usually, at the gentle urging of my husband). I am fortunate to have a good doctor—Charles Tartaglia, M.D., director of student mental health at George- town University—who helps me control and treat my disor- der.

I've decided to speak out partly because my condition is neither dramatic nor debilitating—mental illness doesn't have to be that way. It was this realization that finally gave me the courage to have a child, despite what is known about the genetic link in bipolar disease. But there's another reason why I'm finally telling my secret: I never want my daughter to be embarrassed by my illness. And in order to ask that of her, I need to get over my own embarrassment. I hope my daughter inherits her father's stability, but I also hope she inherits some of my mother's qualities—her intelligence, for example, and her compassion and grace. I know now that I have some wonderful genes to pass along too.

More than Just the "Baby Blues"

Carol Lee Hall

After five years of trying to conceive, Carol Lee Hall and her husband, Ed, finally succeeded and their daughter, Jennifer Elese, was born. Hall expected to be happy caring for her new baby, but instead she felt like she was imprisoned, chained to her baby, and stuck inside her house. Breast-feeding was particularly frustrating for her, since it seemed that whenever she detached Jennifer from her breast and laid her down for a nap, she would cry for more.

Hall was too proud to admit something was wrong and ask for help until she caught herself stepping off a curb without looking, not caring that she might be hit by a car. At that point, she realized that she needed help. She started relying on her faith in God, which had gotten her through a difficult time when her father suffered with cancer, and she began to feel some hope. She took practical steps, such as teaching Jennifer to drink formula from a bottle and relying on other moms for help and support. She learned that having a baby created a kind of crisis for her, and that allowing herself to grieve the freedom and control she had lost helped her to move on and become a happy mother.

Why am I crying so much? Why am I so sad? Tears splattered into the sink full of dirty dishes. I dabbed my eyes with my sleeve as the dishpan filled with soapy water. Having a baby is supposed to be a happy occasion, so why aren't I happy?

Just months before, my husband, Ed, and I'd become the proud parents of Jennifer Elese. After five years of trying to conceive, my family, friends, and colleagues were so happy for us they gave me six baby showers! We went through parenting classes and read several books to prepare us intellectually for raising our baby, but nothing prepared me for the emotional crisis that soon followed.

Depression Began During Nursing

It began with nursing. When I was sure Jennifer was fast asleep, I gently unlatched her from me and laid her down. However, the moment her head touched the mattress, she woke up and started crying. I couldn't stand to let her cry, so I picked her up and started nursing again. After repeating this process over and over with no success, I finally broke down and cried, too.

For the first month of her life, I was home with Jennifer every day. Part of this was due to Chinese tradition (which was to allow the mother to recover from childbirth), and part was to avoid exposing our baby to possible illnesses. I'll never forget what one friend told me: "You'll never be normal again. Get used to it."

Suddenly all my activities revolved around Jennifer's schedule. I couldn't even take a shower unless my husband was home, in case she woke up and needed to be changed or held before I fed her. It seems cruel to compare caring for a baby to being tortured in prison, but that's how I sometimes felt. I was locked up in the house, "breast-cuffed" with sore nipples to a little crying machine.

Despite my difficulties, kissing and cuddling our baby gave me a wonderful feeling inside. I loved little Jennifer very much; I just couldn't stop crying and feeling overwhelmed by sadness.

Receiving Support from Family and Friends

God must have known I'd have such a difficult time adjusting to motherhood because he surrounded me with supportive people. He gave me the most loving husband a woman could ask for. Because Ed saw what a difficult time I was having, he did everything for the baby except breast-feed her.

My mother was helpful, too, and came to stay with me when Ed went on a business trip. While she was visiting, I started crying in the shower one morning, overcome by despair. My mother knocked on the door to see if I was okay. After I assured her I was, she encouraged me to stop breast-feeding so I could have a bit of freedom. I still thought breast-feeding was best for my baby, so I chose not to follow her advice.

When Jennifer was three weeks old, my in-laws came for a visit. Suddenly, I had an irrepressible urge to leave the house since there were enough adults around to handle whatever could come up. I went grocery shopping, and even though I was gone only 30 minutes, I felt so relieved to get out of the house and do something "normal."

I unloaded my emotional burdens on my best friend, Karen, who reminded me all mothers feel overwhelmed at times. Karen assured me I was a good mom. Another friend, Ginger, made sure I ate regularly. Several friends and relatives inquired about my sleeping habits. Everyone tried to help out when they could, but nobody ever suggested I talk about my emotional state with the one person who really could help me: my physician.

Doesn't Consult a Physician

I was loath to discuss my feelings with a physician, even though I cried in front of my daughter's pediatrician and the whole office staff when I brought Jennifer in for her one-month check-up. The doctor called me a few days later to make sure I was okay. He thought I was experiencing post-partum blues that could lead to post-partum depression if my symptoms lasted much longer. He urged me to call if I felt worse. Even though I cried almost every day for the first three months of motherhood, I never called him.

Part of me was too proud to ask for help. I felt bad enough that I couldn't control my daughter's eating and sleeping habits, let alone my own emotions. Seeing a doctor for my problem felt like admitting to failure. And I was afraid if I was diagnosed with an emotional disorder, people would think I was crazy.

Recognizing the Need for Change

Soon after, I went to the grocery store by myself. I was about to cross the parking lot when I thought, I don't care if a car hits me. It would be going so slow, I'd just get hurt and have to stay in bed. Then someone else would have to care for my baby. I stepped off the curb without checking for traffic. While not exactly suicidal, these thoughts certainly weren't normal. Despite my foolish act, I made it safely to my car. Obviously, something needed to change.

Thankfully, God began answering my prayers for strength in some unexpected ways. A friend approached me and said: "My father's dying of cancer. Didn't your father have cancer too? How did you handle it?" I recounted some of my experiences in hopes of comforting her.

That night, while I put my daughter to bed, I thought, If God got me through my father's bout with cancer, surely he can get me through caring for my baby, which is a much happier situation! I sighed in relief, and for the first time felt a glimmer of hope.

Making Some Changes

At her second month check-up, Jennifer's pediatrician said she wasn't gaining enough weight and suggested I supplement breast-feeding with formula. After several attempts, she finally took a bottle and gradually started gaining weight. Slowly I weaned her, and by the fourth month she drank only formula. Not only did this help Jennifer grow, it also freed me from what I thought of as prison.

I gained some control over my daughter's sleeping habits when I "discovered" the pacifier. In the beginning, she wouldn't take it. Later, when she began using a bottle, she readily took the pacifier, too. What a relief! From then on, after feeding her, I gave Jennifer the pacifier and she quietly sucked herself to sleep. Stabilizing her sleeping and eating habits allowed me to regulate my own.

With time, my lifestyle adjusted to include our baby. I learned which department stores had the best diaper changing/nursing areas in their restrooms. At parties, I gratefully "allowed" others to hold Jennifer while I enjoyed refreshments and adult conversation. I interacted with other moms at a women's Bible study and sought their advice on child-rearing. As I became accustomed to the changes in my life, I had less reason to be sad and didn't cry as much.

Understanding What Happened

A few years later, I was asked to lead a Bible study at my church. As part of the training, I was required to read a book and watch a video series entitled Crisis Care by noted Christian counselor H. Norman Wright. In the book he writes, "If you don't recognize something as a loss, then you don't spend time and energy dealing with it and grieving over it." When I read that, my eyes watered because I finally understood what I'd gone through emotionally with my daughter's birth years before.

Until that moment, I never dreamed having a baby was a type of crisis. My parenting books said I'd experience great changes in my life. No one wants to think of having a baby as a loss. Jennifer herself was a gain. But from reading Dr. Wright's book, I discovered I was grieving my loss of control, freedom, and former lifestyle. Realizing this allowed me to grieve consciously and continue to move forward with a healthy, hopeful mindset.

I also learned that another reason I'd felt so blue was because of my fluctuating hormone levels. My family physician eventually explained that after a woman gives birth, her hormones, such as estrogen, and other chemicals, such as seratonin and dopamine (which give the body a sense of well-being), are at low levels. If they're in short supply, situations that wouldn't normally depress a woman might make her feel sad. Lack of sleep and sporadic, sometimes unhealthy, eating habits also can contribute to distress.

Although my bout with post-partum blues resolved itself as time went by, I've wondered what would have happened if I'd been struck by a car in that parking lot. What if my baby hadn't taken a bottle? What if no one had helped me? Looking back, I realize I shouldn't have been embarrassed to discuss my feelings with my doctor. My depression could have gotten worse. Some new mothers with extreme post-partum depression commit suicide and/or infanticide. In retrospect, I would have been better off being fully diagnosed by my physician before the situation could have gotten out of control.

Advice for Other Women

Knowing what I know now, I urge any woman who suspects she might be suffering from depression to seek medical advice as soon as possible. You don't have to display all the symptoms of clinical depression to be considered depressed. Don't be embarrassed that your friends might find out. Don't wait until it gets worse. And if you know someone who might be depressed, urge her to see her doctor—even offer to make the appointment for her and take her there.

When my daughter's grown and perhaps having babies of her own, I know I won't be able to prevent her from going through some of the same difficulties I did. But hopefully if she has a similar experience, she'll be able to talk to me about her feelings and I'll be able to help her the way my mom and

others helped me. And hopefully she'll also be able to confi-
dently rely on God for direction, strength, and peace.

Suddenly Depressed at Forty

Paul Gottlieb

Paul Gottlieb was a competent executive in publishing and considered himself to be happily married. He had never experienced any symptoms of depression. When he was almost forty years old, he was overcome by a sense of dread and found himself breaking into tears for no apparent reason. Dark periods of sleeplessness, worry, and self-doubt haunted him for the next four years. He continued to function in the outside world as if nothing was wrong, but inside he was suffering tremendously.

Gottlieb finally confided in a psychiatrist friend, who prescribed antidepressants and referred him to an analyst for therapy. Neither seemed to help and his condition continued to worsen. Finally, he was referred to a pyschopharmacologist by a friend of his wife and began to get the treatment he needed. The doctor explained that the type of depression Gottlieb was suffering from had causes that were physiological rather than psychological. He experimented until he came up with the right combination of antidepressants to bring Gottlieb out of his depression. After sixteen years, Gottlieb was able to stop his medications and he has not suffered a recurrence.

Birthdays were always marvelous days for me, and they were enthusiastically celebrated in my family. As my fortieth birthday approached, however, I was dreading it for no particular reason. It would have been normal for me to plan a big celebration, but I just didn't want to do it that year. It didn't feel right. My natural emotions were being affected by something I didn't quite understand. In retrospect, I now know that I was experiencing the onset of a severe depression, which lasted from 1974 until 1981.

Paul Gottlieb, *Nothing to Hide: Mental Illness in the Family*. New York: The New Press, 2002. © 2002 by Jean J. Beard and Peggy Gillespie. Reproduced by permission of The New Press, www.thenewpress.com. (800) 233-4830.

I was in what I thought was a happy marriage at the time. I had two wonderful sons. I had a successful career in publishing, which was moving along well. Of course, I had certain frustrations, but they were the normal frustrations of everyday life.

I began to have certain experiences that were very strange and puzzling to me. For example, one day, I was talking to someone at work about a close colleague of mine and I just burst into tears. I remember thinking how odd that was. It wasn't the sort of behavior that was characteristic of me at all.

In thinking about my past, I don't remember demonstrating any symptoms of depression in my childhood or even in my adolescence, when all sorts of difficult things can happen. When I started college, I had just turned seventeen. I was an erratic student, and eventually I got thrown out for being a completely irresponsible character. I had been pretty well-behaved at home, but when I hit college I got a little wild. I was kind of immature and I was drinking and partying more than I should have. But I don't think that was about depression. I think it was about busting loose.

During my college years, I had a roommate who battled with mental illness. He tried to commit suicide and wound up being hospitalized. I was fairly supportive of him, but his struggles didn't resonate or call up any echoes within me at the time. As a matter of fact, until I was hit by depression myself more than twenty years later, I was rather intolerant of people who were unable to deal with their own difficulties. I was the kind of person who would urge someone to pull up their socks and just get on with it. One of my closest friends struggled with depression for years, and I used to get very annoyed with him. I couldn't understand why he was making such a fuss about what I saw as no big deal. . . .

Many years went by, my wife and I had two sons, and all of a sudden it was 1974 and I was about to turn forty. That was when depression began to take over my life. It happened gradually, almost as if it were two steps down, one step back up. It wasn't a direct descent into something; it wasn't like plummeting out of a window.

I've always been a very proud person and a competent, take-charge kind of man. When my depression started, I was running a company in a rather authoritative way. People expected me to be the leader, and I was comfortable with that role. But all of a sudden, things became much more complex, confusing, and difficult for me. I've heard that depression sometimes hits people who seem particularly competent. When you begin to experience depressive periods, there's a sense of guilt and a worry that people are going to discover that you're not the strong person you seem to be. You become riddled with self-doubt.

In the first couple of years of my depression, I grappled alone with disturbing symptoms. I had this feeling of implosion, of everything being sucked in, of the walls closing in. It was as if there were plates in my head, similar to tectonic plates that are always moving and are not together as they should be. I began to lose my ability to easily manage the realities of my life.

Over time, the simplest, most practical things became extremely difficult. Little things became major decisions. For instance, I had trouble picking out a tie in the morning, or I would look at my messy desk and it would terrify me. I would think, "How can I go on like this? How can I go on so ineffectively and inefficiently?" I was worried that everyone would find out I was an empty shell and everything was falling apart inside me. I won't say that every day was like that, but the frequency of days like that accelerated.

I would enter dark periods of sleeplessness, of constant inchoate worry about nothing specific, and of increasing inability to function. My wife was somewhat aware of what I was going through, but I talked to no one about it in detail, including her. I was a responsible, self-sustaining person who did everything for myself. I didn't need anybody to help me. I was the strong one in the family, the "giver" in our marriage. In fact, I was the one who helped everyone else all the time. In a pinch, people called on me. I was reluctant to share my feelings even with my closest friends.

I kept hoping that I would feel better. Whenever my suffering would go away for a week or so, I'd say to myself, "I'm fine. I'm going to be just fine." But over the next four years, matters continued to grow worse. The darkness gathered, and I began to lead a sort of double life. Externally, I "acted" the part of myself in my personal and professional worlds. I knew enough of what my normal behavior had been like before I got sick to act it out. And I wasn't such a bad actor!

I finally got to a point where I was feeling so bad that I turned to my dearest friend, Jeffrey Kramer, who was a brilliant Freudian psychiatrist. I called him up one day and said, "I have to talk to you," and we went out and had lunch. Jeffrey was somebody with whom I had always shared all the adventures of my life, both positive and negative, and he knew more about me than anybody else, except perhaps my wife. Of course, he was upset when I told him what I had been wrestling with for so long. He felt he should have noticed what was happening to me, but I was such a good actor that even Jeffrey hadn't been able to see it. Certainly, he hadn't been looking at me with a professional analytical eye. His reaction was to put me in touch with a well-known Freudian analyst in New York. I saw this psychoanalyst on and off from 1976 until 1981.

Before I began therapy, I felt that I knew myself quite well in all the dark interstices of my mind. Although there were a couple of insights and cathartic moments in therapy, there were no surprises and nothing that I didn't already know. I already understood my relationship with different members of my family, and I sort of understood who I was and what I was about. My treatment didn't touch the core of my increasingly

depressive condition. My analyst was baffled. He didn't understand my case. We examined this and that, but unresolved
psychological issues didn't seem to be the cause of my problem. It was caused by something else, and neither he nor I
knew what it was. Looking back on it all, psychoanalytic treatment was not a totally useless exercise, but it really had nothing to do with my particular kind of depression.

Jeffrey, in consultation with my analyst, would prescribe
rather primitive medications for me. None of the drugs I tried
helped me very much, and I felt increasingly worse. I sometimes suffered side effects such as sexual dysfunction and diz-
ziness, so I stopped taking these drugs on a regular basis.

There were very few days when I couldn't make it to my
office. Working was the one thing that somehow kept me
moving, and I had to earn a living. As bad as it was sitting in
the office and faking everything, it was better than just sitting
at home and staring at the walls around me. But there were
days when it was literally almost impossible to get dressed to
go to work. I was frightened.

Because I'm in the field of art book publishing, I have always led a gregarious and sociable business life. You go to ex-
hibition openings, you have lunch with people, and you attend meetings. I was finding these kinds of activities more and
more difficult to do. There was a time at work when I would
literally hide at lunchtime. I would buy a newspaper, go to a
hotel, find the men's room, lock myself in a stall, and pass the
hour reading the paper in order to stay out of the way of
other people. And then I would have to make myself go back
to work. I couldn't wait to get home at the end of the day and
crawl into bed.

When my psychic pain became unrelenting, I began to
have suicidal thoughts. At a certain point, you weigh the misery that you feel against the positive aspects of your life. I still
had a wife and two children whom I loved, but it was as if the
balance was shifting the other way. The desire to relieve myself

of my pain became more and more intense. All the reasons for living—my sons, the rest of my family, my friends, my enthusiastic engagement with the world around me—were now outweighed by excruciating mental suffering. The pain had simply grown too great.

Even though I loved my sons, I began to think they would be better off without me because I was going to become a terrible burden to them. I never actually tried to commit suicide, but I played "toreador" with buses. I would cross the street in the most dangerous ways possible, sort of tempting fate to knock me down. When I was in my office, I would sometimes sit at my desk, stare out the window, and contemplate jumping.

Things got so bad that I could no longer hide the intensity of my condition from my wife, but she wasn't capable of dealing with it. Instead, she was frightened and angry and couldn't talk about it with me. I suppose from her perspective she felt cheated out of what she had learned to expect from her husband, which was a certain kind of behavior and a certain kind of reality. Our marital life was disintegrating.

The weird thing was that through all of this I was still running companies. In the earliest days of my illness in 1975, I was the CEO of a company called American Heritage Publishing Company. Then I founded the U.S. branch of a British publishing company, a very successful enterprise, which I ran until 1979. In 1980, I was invited to come to Harry N. Abrams Inc. as editor in chief, and I accepted that post. It was a big job with new responsibilities, and yet, I was getting sicker and sicker. In spite of everything, I was still able to perform well enough to be appointed president of Abrams within the year. I felt as if I was digging my nails into the palms of my hands, continuing to function with a sort of stubborn determination.

Things continued to get worse for me emotionally. One day, I literally couldn't get myself to go to work. Instead, I rented a car and drove from Manhattan up to West Point and just walked around. I felt lost and separated from life. It was ghastly. When I was driving back home to the city, I stopped on the New Jersey side of the Hudson River just above the George Washington Bridge and stood at the edge of the cliffs overlooking the river. I don't remember if I was seriously thinking of hurling myself down. I don't even know if I could have done it. But I started screaming hysterically. Screaming. Just screaming into the air. I was desperate.

I don't know how, but I managed to get through that fall and winter at work. By this time, I was the CEO at Abrams as well as the publisher. When you think about it, it's really crazy that you can be that sick and fool everybody. It was an act; a very effective acting job. Sometimes people who appear competent and accomplished find it very difficult to admit that they've become weak and disabled. If you have the means, as I did, to fake it, well, you fake it. You're in denial. But you don't even know exactly what you're denying.

On April Fool's Day 1981, I went to work as usual. By noon, I was in such a state that I knew I had to leave the office and that I couldn't come back. The pain had grown too great, and I was having constant suicidal thoughts. I was breaking down. I started walking across Central Park toward my analyst's office, and I remember feeling as if I were walking barefoot on broken glass. Every step I took was excruciatingly painful.

When I got to my analyst's office, I hammered on his door, and of course he was startled to see me show up there without an appointment. He took one look at me and immediately called my wife. He told her that I was having a complete breakdown and needed to be institutionalized. After my wife got off the phone with my analyst, she got a call from a friend of hers. My wife blurted out what was going on with me. By a miraculous coincidence, it turned out that this friend had a relative who was a psychopharmacologist. I was able to get an appointment to see this doctor the very next morning.

In the meantime, my analyst just wanted to get rid of me. He was finished. He couldn't do anything more for me. Whatever he'd been doing was like applying a Band-Aid to a severed aorta. I crawled out of his office, went to a phone, and told my wife that I would meet her at Jeffrey's house. I managed to get myself to his place, and I just lay down on the floor. My wife came to get me and somehow we made it home.

The next morning, I met with the psychopharmacologist, a knowledgeable scientist and sympathetic doctor. He gave me hope for the first time in six years. He explained that I had an endogenous depression, meaning that I was depressed for physiological rather than psychological reasons. He told me that he would find the right combination of drugs, which could cure my illness and end my misery. These were his words to me: "You're going to be fine. Your sickness is not unlike diabetes. It's as if something is wrong with your blood. I don't know what it is yet, but I'm going to find your insulin."

I told the doctor, "I can't go on. I've got to call my company and resign. I can't take the pressure of it. I can't cope anymore. I need to be institutionalized." He replied, "No you don't. Don't make any decisions yet. Do not resign." I decided to take his advice, but I didn't go back to the office. The doctor and I cooked up the notion that I had developed diverticulitis, and that I was going to be hospitalized for observation. No one except my wife was allowed to visit me.

I spent about a week in the hospital, where I sank into a kind of oblivion while my doctor experimented with various antidepressant drugs. He explained that with mental illness, you can't just draw a blood sample and say, "Ah-ha! You need this, or you need that."

People have many different kinds of experiences with mental illness. My doctor posited that at one end of the scale there are those who are suffering from psychological problems generated by relationship or parenting issues or whatever, and at the other end are people who are purely physiologically ill. I seemed to be in the latter category, because at the end of the period of experimentation the doctor finally mixed the right cocktail of medications for me. Miraculously, I was "myself" again, and after that, I never experienced a moment of the old depression.

I was basically cured and I went back to work. It was as if the mist had cleared and there I was again. During all those years of my illness, there was the reality of my internal mind and then there was my external performance in the world. The combination of drugs somehow brought my interior and exterior selves back together. There were no more tectonic plates shifting around in my head.

If I hadn't found a doctor who cured me, I would have died. I think I would have killed myself. Fortunately, human beings can't really remember pain, but we can sort of put ourselves back in the memory of the emotional state we were in. As I look back now on that time in my life, it was unbearable. When life becomes unbearable, people kill themselves. Even though there are all the reasons in the world to stay alive, there are also overwhelming feelings that you can't go on anymore. It's like drowning. You are suffocated by them.

Once the doctor felt that I was in good shape, he took me off all my medications and prescribed a very small dose of lithium as a maintenance drug. He thought it was necessary, and I accepted his decision. It was amazing to feel better again but at first it was scary, because I thought, "Will this cure last?" My doctor warned me to be on guard. "You could get into a depressed period again or you could become manic-depressive," he said. "You must not forget what happened to you."

After twenty-nine years of marriage, my wife and I divorced. I know that my illness had a destructive impact on our marriage, although her behavior and interests had a great deal to do with it as well. If she were a different kind of person, it might have turned out differently, but because my illness was so very frightening for her, she was not supportive of me in any important way. Instead of being responsive, my wife pursued her own interests even more vigorously than before, and her career became more and more significant for her. She and I never really faced what was going on with me, partly because neither of us understood it for such a long time. I certainly didn't understand it. She was neither able to understand it, nor was she of a mind to try very hard. Her escape from my illness was to escape from our marriage.

After my marriage ended, I soon fell in love with the compassionate, smart, and beautiful woman who has been my wife ever since. I've never been happier. I fell in love with her the first time we went out, and by our second date, I thought I had to tell her about my depression. After we came home that evening, I put out a bottle of port, most of which I drank, and I told her everything. Fortunately, she has a Zen-like kind of spirit and she accepts things as they are.

If I were to distinguish between two major groups of people, there are those who have endured some kind of adversity and there are those who haven't. The latter spend most of their lives worrying about how they will survive if something bad happens to them. If you are in the large group who has suffered some adversity, whether physical or mental, you may learn, as Roosevelt said, "There's nothing to fear but fear itself." In fact, there's nothing to fear but death itself. If you can make it through a really bad time and survive, nothing can get you.

I decided a few years ago that it might be time to go off the small maintenance dose of lithium I had been taking for sixteen years. I went to my psychopharmacologist and said, "Enough already. I feel great." I had felt great for years. That's not to say that I couldn't feel sad or depressed. I had lived through the death of a father I adored and the death of a marriage that I thought I was in for life, with appropriate feelings of grief and sadness that eventually evaporated. You go back to your life. It's not unlike the attack on the World Trade Center on September 11. You feel horrible, then you wake up one day and say, "I don't have an option. I have to keep on going." At any rate, my doctor said he didn't recommend going off lithium, because the fact was that nobody knew what could happen. He advised me not to fix something that was working so well. He thought that if I went off it, another problem might be triggered and he might not be able to pull me out the same way he had before. So I continued to take the medication.

In 1997, my publishing company was sold to a French corporation. I was under tremendous stress and I felt anxious and exhausted. All of a sudden, I developed a variety of symptoms, including blurred vision, insomnia, lack of physical coordination, mental confusion, slurred speech, and hand tremors. I even lost twenty-six pounds in six weeks. It was a nightmare. At first, I assumed the symptoms were related to the pressures of work. Well, they weren't.

Over the years, it never would have occurred to me that the small dose of lithium I was taking might be poisoning me. My doctor had never told me that when you take lithium your blood levels have to be monitored on a regular basis. I wasn't told that lithium is one of those drugs with a narrow "window" of effectiveness: Too little is useless, and too much can kill you. It's a very volatile drug. For whatever reason, in the spring of 1997, I had a severe toxic reaction to the lithium. Very few people had taken it every day for sixteen years, so it may have been a cumulative effect, or maybe my body chemistry had changed.

Perhaps I should have taken more responsibility for my own physical state. If you take any drug, obviously you should question its power, the reasons for its prescription, and insist on knowing all possible side effects on both a short- and a long-term basis. You should be warned to watch for specific symptoms and deal with them as soon as possible. I realize now that my childish faith in all doctors is a product of a different time.

By the time my blood levels were tested, I had lost two-thirds of my kidney function. As soon as I stopped taking the lithium, I recovered completely and began to feel better physically than I had in years. Fortunately, going off lithium did not plunge me back into the dark night of depression.

I haven't been on any medication since 1997. None. Zero. So far, so good. Who knows, I may be sailing through a benign period and then in a year, I may just crash off the face of the earth. But I will be watching out for this and I will not forget what it felt like to be so sick.

When I was ill, I would look at my friends who had some kind of spiritual and religious faith and envy them because I saw that it gave them a certain solace or comfort. And yet, I've never been drawn to religion and I don't have any sense of a need for it. I grew up in a totally secular family. My mother, who is going on ninety-one, is an atheist. She came out of the old leftist philosophy that says, "Religion is the opiate of the masses." Although we're Jews, I grew up without any feelings of identification with any kind of religion. I do believe in the basic human tenet of "Do unto others." That makes sense to me. And I do have a belief in the possible goodness of men and women, and in the joy that life and the world can bring us.

My struggle with depression has made me available and sympathetic to people who are troubled. I can see them a mile away. There's an artist, a young woman, who came into my office one day with a project to discuss. I looked at her and asked, "Are you all right?" She just fell apart. It turned out that she had been struggling for years with depression and she couldn't talk to her parents about it. I was the first person who had identified something that was crushing her. She went on to get treatment, although she still struggles with the demon of depression.

People have learned an awful lot about mental illness in the past twenty years, but I still think it is highly stigmatized in the business world. When I was running Abrams, we were a subsidiary of a $4 billion corporation that installed a personnel policy for screening new employees for alcohol and drug abuse. I argued with the medical director of the corporation, saying, "I don't care if people are abusing drugs or alcohol, the real root cause for many of them is probably depression. They're self-medicating as a way of trying to mask something they don't understand. That is the problem you should be focusing on." When I disagreed with him about the company's policy, he had no idea that I was suffering from depression myself.

People say that more man-hours are lost in the work environment from unidentified and untreated depression than from all other illnesses combined. Where I worked, if you had a heart problem or cancer, you'd never find a more sympathetic, supportive group of people and medical programs. But for years I had to be secretive about my mental illness because I was in control of millions of dollars of the corporation's assets, and I couldn't run the risk of having my judgment mistrusted.

This past year, I was interviewed by the *Wall Street Journal* for an article about executives who suffer from depression. When the article ran, I didn't get any negative responses. Instead, I received many letters and messages applauding what I had done and telling me, "Yes, I have suffered from depression, too, and have never spoken of it." Some of the most amazing responses I've had were from colleagues and friends whose stories I never would have guessed. They were "acting" at the same time as I was "acting," and we never knew about each other's suffering.

The statistic I've heard is that something like 30 million people in this country suffer from depression, and thirty thousand people a year commit suicide. There's a huge population suffering from this illness.

In the business environment, it's very important to spread the notion that even people who are in the grip of this disease can and do function. Most people who are successful aren't likely to talk about a history with mental illness. First of all, there's the stigma. Second of all, there's a kind of hubris in one's success, and one doesn't want to redirect attention to something that is the antithesis of success. It's important to realize that mental illness is not a failure; it's a life horror.

Life is weird, isn't it? I had dinner last Saturday night with an old friend. We'd been through our "life wars" together, and I said to him, "Life is just a big soap opera. We're in it. We still have parts. And we can't change the channel."

SOCIAL ISSUES
FIRSTHAND

CHAPTER 2

Living with Depression

Depression Progresses Gradually—and So Does Recovery

Michele Capots and Erica Lumiere

In this article, Michele Capots describes her descent into depression and the long road back to normalcy. In her position as a newspaper reporter, Capots found herself working twelve-hour days. She began feeling tired and moody, but at first blamed these feelings on her job. Over a period of months, the feelings got worse and she experienced insomnia and loss of appetite and started obsessing over the sense of feeling like a failure. Looking out her window on what others would have considered to be a beautiful day, she realized how miserable she was feeling.

She drove to her mother's house for help. Her mother immediately took her to see the family doctor, who diagnosed her as clinically depressed. He prescribed antidepressant medications and therapy, Capots took a leave of absence from her job, expecting to feel better in a matter of weeks. Instead, it was several brutal months before she felt the blackness lifting and was able to go back to work. A second bout with depression was easier for her to handle, as she recognized the symptoms and consulted her doctor immediately. At the time this article was written, five years after her original diagnosis, Capots had a positive attitude about life and hope that her depression would not return.

The day was gorgeous, one of those "I cannot believe how beautiful it is out" spring days that make you glad to be alive. It was May 1996, and as I looked out my bedroom window at the park across the street, I studied people enjoying the day. There was a young couple sitting on a blanket, having a romantic picnic under a tree. There was a jogger running with his black Lab. To the left, there was a little girl sweetly offering her mother a lick of her melting mess of an ice-cream cone. And the only thing running through my brain was, I hate all of you.

They were happy; I was not. They were experiencing everyday joy, something I could no longer even remember. Over the past six months, I had watched helplessly as my life disintegrated around me. Over and over again, I asked myself the same questions: Why was I mad at the world? Why did I feel so down, so hopeless? What was wrong with me?

Two weeks later, I made the hour-long drive to visit my mother. She took one look at me and knew something was terribly wrong. I fell into her arms, sobbing, and begged her to help me.

Depression Creeps Up Slowly

Depression doesn't hit you all at once, like a speeding Mack truck. It's far more subtle—and sinister—than that. It's a disease, one that creeps up on you slowly until it feels like a constant, crushing weight. Before my meltdown in my mother's arms, I'd had no idea I was so far gone.

I'd attributed my increasing moodiness to being worn out from the stress of working 12-hour days as a newspaper reporter. But after a few months, I knew it was something beyond simple fatigue. At first, I lost my appetite. Then, insomnia set in. I would lay in bed and stare at the ceiling, a voice in my head taunting me, saying I was a failure. I obsessed over the fact that my friends were getting promoted and engaged and buying houses while I was languishing in my career, barely able to make the rent. On top of that, my boyfriend was moving across the country—and I didn't know if I wanted to be in a long-distance relationship.

I managed to keep my act together in public for a while. But eventually, my bout with the blues began affecting my work. That's when I knew I was in trouble. I zoned out at meetings; while taking notes, my hands would shake uncontrollably. I couldn't make the simplest decisions; I found myself spending an hour in the mornings just trying to figure out what to wear to work.

Everyday tasks overwhelmed me, I also felt paranoid. Every time I heard laughter in the office, I was convinced someone was making jokes about me. The minute my shift was over, I'd rush home to my apartment, needing the closed door to feel safe.

Seeking Help

This went on for two months before that day I drove to my mom's. That very afternoon, she whisked me to our family doctor, who diagnosed me as clinically depressed. I was skeptical. To me, depression was something that happened to older people. "I'm just in a funk," I said. "I can't be depressed. I'm only 25!"

He prescribed three medications: Prozac for depression, Xanax for anxiety, and Trazodone to help me sleep through the night. He also insisted that I see a therapist and take time off from work. While I didn't think it was necessary, I agreed to two weeks of sick leave.

No Quick Cure

My hopes for a quick cure did not materialize. By the end of the two weeks, I could barely drag myself out of bed, much less get out of my ratty pajamas or take a shower. All I wanted to do was sleep. And there was a new, even more terrifying turn: I began to fantasize about killing myself.

By this point, my best friend, Jennifer, and my mother were desperately worried. Depression didn't run in my family, but my mom knew my childhood wasn't exactly easy. My father died of a heart attack at the age of 35 while playing basketball. I was just a toddler then, so my memories of him are from photos. But I missed him dearly. Since we had only each other, my mom and I were very close. She remarried when I was 17, which was a big adjustment, but I was thrilled. Then, unbelievably, my new stepfather died just six months later. Somehow, I managed to bury my grief and move on.

When my mother learned my "quarter-life crisis" was causing me to have suicidal thoughts, she didn't trust me to be alone. And, truth be told, neither did I. So, in August, we decided it was best for me to give up my apartment and move back home with her.

Every morning, as soon as I opened my eyes, I'd pull the covers over my head and cry. Why weren't my medications working their magic? I got angry when Mom opened the blinds to let the sunlight in: I wanted the room dark, like I felt inside. She begged me to get out of bed, and I hated seeing how scared she was. But all I wanted was to disappear.

The Long Road to Recovery

Looking back now, I realize that I hadn't been prepared for how long it takes depression to leave you, and how brutal the fight against it can be. It was another two months before I really started to feel the benefits of the pills, like a slow awakening, and finally felt as if my weekly therapy sessions were leading me out of the blackness. I started taking long walks and even grabbed an occasional cup of coffee with a friend.

On my first day back at work in November, I was a wreck: Most of my colleagues knew about my meltdown, and I was ashamed. But when I walked into my office, I was greeted by a huge bouquet of flowers on my desk with a card that read, WELCOME BACK.

Everyone tried to make me feel like things were back to normal again, but I knew that my life was forever changed. People watched what they said and did around me, as if I might lose it at any given moment. My boss offered to lighten my workload, but I insisted that he treat me the same as he did before my breakdown. I was determined to break free of my depression and pull my life back together, even if it meant being on medication and seeing a therapist for the rest of my life.

It took another few months before I fully felt like myself again. The following year, I moved out of my mother's house and in with a roommate. I wanted to prove that I was strong enough to live on my own, but secretly, I was terrified. I'd heard that up to 60 percent of people with depression have a relapse within two years. And I did relapse. But luckily, my second bout with depression wasn't nearly as severe—partly because I knew the way back out of that black hole. I recognized the signs early on and got help right away. I stepped up my therapy and had my medication monitored more closely until I was in the clear.

Today, I'm still in therapy, and I still take Prozac, though my doctors are slowly weaning me off both. And you know what? My life is working. I have a super-supportive new boyfriend and an amazing group of friends. I've also learned to consider my successes as well as my failures. I just turned 30, and for the first time, I actually like myself. I can't explain it, but I feel so incredibly lucky about what I have. Do I think I will ever get depressed again? I can't say no, but I hope not. I'm trying to put the bad times behind me, because I know there's so much to look forward to.

Depressed Since the Fourth Grade

Cathy Poor

In this article Cathy Poor recalls her history of depression, beginning when she was in the fourth grade and experiencing extreme emotional swings and bouts of crying that went on for weeks. Her symptoms continued to worsen until she was a junior in high school, attending a boarding school. After two major episodes where she fell apart and had to be sent home, school staff sent her to a psychiatrist. She was diagnosed with clinical depression, put on medication, and began to feel better.

During Poor's freshman year of college, depression descended again and she found herself spending hours crying every day. She spoke to very few friends about what was going on, but relied on her mom for support. Her mom helped her to get back on her medications and become stable again.

WHEN I WAS A JUNIOR IN HIGH SCHOOL, I was diagnosed with clinical depression. Everyday living turned into a challenge for me. Things as simple as eating or getting dressed in the morning were difficult, much less having the concentration to do my schoolwork. Given what I know now about depression, my symptoms could have been creeping up on me as early as elementary school.

From the fourth grade on, I experienced extreme emotional swings and an unusually strong attachment to certain people. I was ten when I broke up with my "boyfriend," and I cried and cried for weeks. I didn't know why I was crying so much, since he hadn't really been a significant part of my life. My mom had to take me to work with her because l was emotionally out of control. In eighth grade, I became so attached to one particular teacher that I never wanted to leave her classroom. I dreaded the end of the school year. Since I've been in treatment, some of these desperate feelings have lessened.

I left home to go to boarding school in the ninth grade. Soon after I arrived, I went through two waves of bad depression and I had trouble eating and sleeping. In my sophomore year, I had my first overt breakdown. I was in a diving meet. When I made my first dive and didn't do it perfectly; I totally lost it. I started to cry and I couldn't stop. When I went back to my dorm that night, I still couldn't pull myself back together. The next week was exam week, and my mom had to come take me home because I was falling apart. Luckily, my teachers let me take my exams at home. I returned to school when the exam period ended, and I was able to complete the year.

In my junior year, I was in trouble from the start. Once again, I had difficulty eating and sleeping. I was living in a dorm, but I isolated myself from my peers. I didn't go out, and I spent most of my time alone. I was ashamed because I thought that my feelings of depression were caused by a lack of strength or will on my part. I wanted to suck it up and get through it by myself.

I broke down again during exam week just as I had the year before. When I had to leave school a second time, the staff said, "This issue has to be addressed." They referred me to a psychiatrist, who diagnosed me with clinical depression.

I felt like I was finally being taken care of. The school had stepped in and said, "All right, this is what we're going to do, and this is what you have to do." It was out of my hands, and I was relieved because I didn't have to manage everything on my own anymore. Once my school got involved, I felt like I could let myself go and just be me. School became a safety net that was there to catch me.

I only told two other people besides my mom and my therapist about my situation. One was a girl who had gone to my school the year before, and the other was one of my teachers. They were both incredibly good listeners and very supportive. They didn't try to "fix" me. They simply let me be me and say what I wanted to say. You can be irrational when you're depressed, and they understood that.

After I was diagnosed, I was put on medication. I began to feel much better and was able to finish my high school education. When I graduated, I assumed that I would get well because I was away from the social and academic pressures of school. I guess I still wasn't willing to admit that my depression wasn't circumstantial. I didn't want to believe that there was something wrong with me. I preferred to blame my environment for causing my problems. Being strong-willed and stubborn, I decided to go off my medication.

My first term at college was miserable, and I had my worst bout of depression yet. Besides the emotional strain, I wasn't able to eat or sleep at all, and I had a lot of physical pain as well. I felt like I had a huge lump in my chest that I couldn't get rid of. It was almost impossible to swallow, and there was nothing I could do about it. When I was studying, I was so tense that I felt like screaming or kicking something really hard. I felt as if my muscles were going to jump out of my skin.

I went to all of my classes, but I could only concentrate on one course at a time. Each week, I prioritized my four courses and picked one that would get my full attention. All the rest, I let slide. Given the circumstances, I did pretty well academically. I don't know why, but there was something about working against the odds that inspired me to do the best I could.

During my daily routine of academics and athletics, I had to fit in about two hours of total dysfunction. I would sit in the library and study for a while and then I would cry. I would call my mom and bawl over the phone, or go for a walk and cry.

I was socially isolated during my freshman year. I had two roommates, but I never told them what was happening to me. I would never break down in front of them. I was always in a nook by myself in the library where I could quietly fall apart. I'd call my mom from a phone in the basement. I think my roommates may have suspected that something was wrong, but they never brought it up.

I felt comforted when I called my mom, but it was a double-edged sword. She provided a huge amount of support, but because I knew I had her support, I would let myself fall apart even more. If I was sitting in the library about to cry, and I knew that my mother wasn't available to speak to me, I would try harder to keep myself together. If, on the other hand, I knew that I could reach her, I would let myself go. My crying episodes would stop after a certain amount of time, so it was just a matter of weathering them when they happened. Even though they would get worse when I talked to my mom, she would always weather them with me.

At first, I was so ashamed of my tears that I would try not to cry, or would only let myself cry for half an hour or so. If I did cry, I would reprimand myself the entire time, thinking, "This is terrible. You are so weak." I felt guilty whenever I called my mom, because she would get so upset when she heard me sounding so miserable. But she had told me that she wanted me to call her whenever I needed to. She wanted to know how I was doing. This was comforting and eased some of the guilt I felt. It showed me the extent of her love. She was willing to suffer in order to help me.

One time when I was having a good day, I called my mom to show her that I was actually happy for once. That afternoon, I lost it again and I just didn't have the heart to call her back. I wanted to give her a day off. Instead, I called one of my old friends to weather the episode with me, but it was clear that she really didn't get it. Normally, if you call someone and you're crying they'll say, "What's wrong?" And if you can't really explain what's wrong, then you sort of look around for something else to say to them, like, "Oh, well, I have a test tomorrow and I'm nervous about it." Then they might say, "Okay, how are you going to study for this test?" And they'll try to strategize and make it all better, but depression is not a rational thing. Most people don't understand it, which is why I don't tell too many of my friends about my illness.

My mom is someone who does get it. She has never said to me, "Why are you doing this?" She has always said, "Okay, well, this is what we're going to do about it. I'm going to call the physician and we're going to get you back on medication, and dah-dah-dah-dah." She would also talk to me about my cats and other stuff that would make me smile. I'm lucky to have someone who truly understands. It's been just the two of us—me and Mom—for a while now.

Keeping Faith While Living with Depression

Renee Schafer Horton

At the time this article was written in 2006, Renee Schafer Horton had been in treatment for depression for over twenty years. Her illness is partially responsive to medication, but she longs for a complete cure. A devout Roman Catholic, Horton pleads with God for a cure, but none is forthcoming.

Speaking from her own experience and from that of others like her, Horton considers the relationship between spirituality and depression. She talks about the difficulty of maintaining one's faith when depressed, the help received from a faith community, and quotes statistics showing that deeply religious people recover from depression more quickly. She also talks about the negative effects of faith, such as feeling abandoned or punished by God. She concludes that the most important characteristic of depressed believers is that they look at life as a gift, even when enduring suffering.

"Is there anything else I can do for you?"

The bank teller was cheerful, as bank tellers tend to be, and the cheerfulness grated; it was too much, too early in the day.

"No, thank you," I said, folding my deposit slip and turning to face the door, spying the people winding their way through the guidance ropes like a giant snake across my path. I concentrated on sending a "Walk to the car" message from my head to my feet, and moved toward the exit. By the time I'd taken the 43 steps from the teller to my waiting vehicle, I was exhausted. I heaved myself into my van, leaned against the steering wheel and wondered how many times I'd heard that question from people in the service industry: "Is there anything else I can do for you?" Hundreds, probably. And each time I say "No, thank you," even though I want to beg, "Yes, actually, there's one more thing: Can you get me a new brain?"

Is Depression a Sin?

In any one-year period, according to the National Institute of Mental Health, about 20.9 million American adults suffer from what the Desert Fathers originally considered one of the seven deadly sins: the sin of sadness. In the 17th century, sadness was dropped from the list, replaced by the sin of sloth, something depressed people often see as ironic since sadness often leads to sloth.

There are a number of varieties of depression, and in the overall scheme, I have a "good" kind because it is partially responsive to medication. I'm overly sensitive to side effects, ruling out complete classes of drugs; others cause "Danger, Will Robinson!" symptoms such as facial tics. Still, following 20 years of treatment, I do not yet fall into hell, which I define as the 15 to 20 percent of people for whom no medication works.

One would think I should rejoice in this good fortune, but I don't. Normally a generous person—giving away my husband's raises, taking in strangers, cooking meals for pregnant women—I become greedy where depression is concerned. I want a cure, and I want it now. I don't want to end up like my mother and uncle, both so engulfed by darkness that they mistook suicide for the light at the end of the tunnel. I don't want to, as my friend Paul once wrote, "join the ranks of the souls with broken hearts that got away when the rest of us weren't looking."

Praying for a Cure

So, I beseech God for a cure, throwing myself at the Almighty's feet. And often, I come up empty, angry, disheartened. Believing in something you cannot see—the very definition of faith—is difficult enough when all your neurotransmitters are lined up like well-behaved Catholic schoolchildren. When the brain's chemical balance is upset, an overwhelming angst sets in, and belief is problematic. One question becomes paramount: Where is God?

Connecting Spirituality and Depression

Although studies have shown a positive connection between spirituality and a lessening of depression, it is frequently difficult for people in the throes of the illness to access their faith, even if they are lifelong believers.

Dick Rice, 64, has had three major bouts of depression over the past 30 years. His first came three decades ago, following missionary work in Calcutta, India.

"There is some truth to the saying that depression is anger turned inward," said Rice, who has been a spiritual director for 35 years and is currently the director of spiritual development at The Retreat in Wayzata, Minn. "My anger was toward God because of Calcutta. At one point after I left, I was skiing and fell on a hill and cried to God, 'Goddamn it, I have nowhere else to go and even if I see no evidence of your care, I believe.' When I took that leap, God caught me and I touched a God who was deeper than I yet believed in."

Kathy Neal, a 57-year-old freelance writer in Little Rock, Ark., had a similar experience. A convert to Catholicism at 18, Neal has suffered from depression for much of her life. She never completely lost faith, but her spiritual practice had to change to accommodate her illness.

"Don't get me wrong, I love the Roman Catholic church and all the rituals that go with it, but because of depression I isolate, and in that isolation, I developed a much more personal relationship with God," Neal explained. She had the Sacred Heart of Jesus enthroned in her home because she could not manage the strength to go to Mass. "I had to get that close to God in my depression to survive it; I feel almost like Jesus is here in my home."

St. Ignatius of Loyola, the founder of the Society of Jesus, warned his followers in the 16th century about "desolations." These moments, he said, could "lead one toward a lack of faith and leave one without hope and without love. One is completely listless, tepid and unhappy, and feels separated from our Creator and Lord."

For me, depression is not just being without faith and hope, but being unable to recall those virtues ever existed. Did I ever love? Has there ever been any reason to live? People try to comfort me with stories about St. John of the Cross and his dark night, or St. Therese of Lisieux and her repeated depression spells, but somehow, thinking the saints were crazy doesn't help me much.

Having Faith Helps When Coping with Depression

At only 30 years old, Tara Dix Osborne has struggled frequently with depression and has learned that faith is a moment-by-moment decision.

"You choose to trust God, even if you have to make that choice every minute over and over again. And then each minute is a little victory over despair, and you must congratulate yourself for that," the Chicago-based writer said.

The late Pope John Paul II addressed a Vatican health care conference on depression three years ago [2003], and encouraged pastors and their congregations to reach out to depressed believers, helping them regain a sense of God's goodness. It is appropriate advice, experts say.

Support from a Faith Community

"People with a faith practice probably have a community of friends around them, which is a great source of support," said Lawrence Cronin, a Tucson psychiatrist who is also Catholic. "There are many with depression who are quite alienated . . . It would seem they do more poorly, fall between the cracks, so to speak."

I can't imagine how I would have survived my slips into despair sans my parish community. More than once someone has reassured me that they will be a stand-in for my limp faith. My spiritual director, a Jesuit scientist with a wicked sense of humor, keeps me tethered to reality. When I'm depressed, it is just a hop, skip and jump from "Life is good" to "I shouldn't be alive." Engulfed in sadness, I see myself as worthless, lazy, stupid and sinful. These perceptions run through my mind like a hamster on a treadmill. Bill reminds me the hamster isn't real, but God is.

The experience of God-through-others is paramount; believing friends change the low-faith/high-despair ratio of depressed people, helping them see a better tomorrow.

"I believe very strongly that God puts certain people in your life who are Christ-like to help you when you are in the pit of despair," said Peggy Schneider, a 49-year-old Tucson homemaker who has lived with depression for nearly a decade. "We still live in a society where there's a stigma about depression. If you have people to turn to who can offer comfort—especially if they have battled depression themselves—it helps you get through the bad days."

Even if one is alienated from friends in depression, however, faith can make a positive difference.

Results of a Recent Study

One of the most recent studies on the intersection of spirituality and depression was published in the April 2006 issue of the *American Journal of Psychiatry*. Duke University researcher

Harold Koenig followed depressed patients for nearly a year after release from hospitals for treatment of medical conditions such as heart disease and stroke. He found that the stronger people's "intrinsic religiosity" score, the faster they recovered from depression. Specifically, Koenig discovered that for every 10-point increase in a person's intrinsic religiosity measurement, there was a 70-percent increase in the speed of recovery from depression. Intrinsic religiosity was defined as a "deep, internally motivated type of religious commitment, related to, but distinct from, organized religious activities and private meditation or prayer." Essentially, people's internal belief helped pull them out of depression.

Osborne said her experience confirms this.

"Being raised on faith has allowed me to hold on," she said: "This isn't to say I feel completely safe in the arms of God when I'm depressed. I still have moments when I feel abandoned by God. But, in my mind I tell myself to trust there will be better days. I have that inner belief that there will be and without faith, I don't think it would be there."

Sometimes Faith Has a Negative Effect

Of course, faith is not a panacea, as any depressed person who's tried to get well on scripture alone will confess. And sometimes, it can have a negative effect.

"Some faithful are rather rigid people, introverted, hard on themselves, unforgiving (including of themselves)," psychiatrist Cronin wrote in an e-mail. "And, of course, they can, just as much as anyone, become delusional with depression and begin to think strange things like God wants them dead. . . . That's [a] reason for positive, uplifting faith, not the punitive type."

Believing in a Loving God

Remaking their image of God from punishing to ever-loving is an important step for many people with depression. I wrestled with that for some time, before accepting that God loved me even when I was angry. Since then, I've been yelling at God on a regular basis. In fact, I pray as though he is deaf, thinking maybe my prior requests were not understood. HERE, I scream, LET ME MAKE MYSELF CLEAR: HEAL ME. Then, knowing the track record on that prayer has been poor, I switch tactics: Please, I beg, don't let my children get depression; protect them from the trauma of watching their mother in illness.

Friends claim I worry too much about this, saying children learn positive virtues such as compassion and perseverance from watching parents battle chronic illnesses. Hogwash, I said. Then my daughter proved them right.

She was only 13 at the time, and I thought I'd been hiding my suffering well. Then I went to my office late one evening and found a note taped to my computer monitor: "Dear Mommy, I love you very much. During this difficult time, I want you to remember that." She had carpeted my keyboard with 10 holy cards of saints, a child's version of bargaining with God for her mother's sanity.

My worst visit from Demon Depression came last April, following a trip to Paris. For reasons I still do not understand, I came home convinced there was no God. It is one thing to think God doesn't hear you; it is quite another to think God doesn't exist.

I made an emergency visit to my psychiatrist, running through a box of tissues in less than 10 minutes. He appeared confused; I'd been fine two months ago when he'd last seen me. What, he asked, had happened?

"I'm not sure," I sobbed, "but I don't think I believe in God anymore."

Dan looked at me for a minute then did something uncharacteristic: He let his brotherly, Jewish side overrule his by-the-book doctor persona. "That's OK," he said, "because God believes in you."

In the end, what saves depressed believers is not doctors and medication, although both are often necessary. Neither is it a Pollyanna-ish belief that "perfect" faith brings healing. What separates believers who thrive in spite of depression from those who don't is something else. It is a concentrated effort to focus on life—even a life of suffering as a gift. In making that effort, they step closer to the Love that believes in us all.

Depression and Race

Meri Nana-Ama Danquah

When Meri Nana-Ama Danquah began reading books about depression, it seemed to her that they were all about white Jewish women from Boston. A few were about white people who were not Jewish women, but there were none about black people like her. She wondered why there weren't any black people writing their stories, as their white counterparts had done. Having experienced signs of depression all her life, she could identify with the inner experiences of the white people, but the similarities didn't extend far enough outward to touch her flesh, the color of her skin.

In this essay, Danquah talks about her decision to write a book herself and explores the relationship between depression and race. She differentiates between clinical depression and the generalized feeling of despair that black women often feel in reaction to the hardships they endure and the expectations placed on them by those around them. She notes how difficult it is for a black woman to separate these, to recognize and admit to depression as a psychological illness, and to be willing to undergo treatment.

For a period of time after clinical depression became the literary topic du jour, it seemed as if most of the work I read about the illness was written by white Jewish women from Boston who had, at some point in their lives, been treated at McLean [a psychiatric hospital in Massachusetts]. I must admit, I always thought it rather odd that one city could contain so much sadness, that one hospital could contain so many talented and successful people among its roster of former patients. Nevertheless, I would search for these books.

Meri Nana-Ama Danquah, *Unholy Ghost: Writers on Depression.* New York: Harper-Collins Publishers, 2001. Copyright © 2001 by Nell Casey. Reproduced by permission of the editor and the author.

I would purchase each and every one as soon as they were published, take them home, and sit barefoot and cross-legged on my couch, with a box of Kleenex at my side, while I read about the lives of these people in this city that systematically manufactured great writers and even greater misery.

As a reader, what I cherish most about literature is the permission it grants me to escape the confines of my own life. No matter who or what I am, have been, or want to be, I am able, for the length of a book, to inhabit a new reality, one that the author constructs. My relationship to the literature of depression, however, is somewhat different. It is based not on a desire to lose myself in the pages of a book, but on a relentless need to find, and define, a very specific part of myself through the book. That part which melancholy stalks like a jealous lover. For many years, the only place in this huge world of words where it appeared as if I was welcome to carry out that search was inside the narratives of these women. These white Jewish women from Boston.

Of course, not all of the work on depression was written by them. During the period of time to which I am referring, a number of authors were writing of madness, of disorders and moods. There were a few books and essays by men and other women, some of whom were not Jewish and did not come from or live anywhere near New England. Regardless of their gender or place of origin, these writers did have one thing in common: they were white. All of them. Which placed me in the peculiar position of having very little choice but to look to these white people for some sense of validation, some basic understanding of who I am as a depressive and, ultimately, as a person underneath this illness.

There are times when I feel like I've known depression longer than I've known myself. It has been with me since the beginning, I think. Long before I learned to spell my name. No, even longer than that. I'm sure that before I could even speak my own name or learn to love the color of my skin, this hollow heartache was following me, patiently awaiting the inevitable crossing of our paths, planning my future unhappiness. I've always been aware that something in my life was not quite right, if not totally wrong. My scales were never balanced. For every twelve joys, I had twenty-five sorrows. And each sorrow was like a song. A melodious seduction bringing me closer and closer to this terrible sickness which has cost me lovers and friendships, money and opportunities, time and more time. So much wasted time.

At first, I had a hard time figuring out why there were no glossy magazine articles or literary books about depression by black people. I've never thought of myself as average, but I've also never thought of myself as an anomaly. Surely there were other black women suffering from depression, questioning their sanity, searching for an affirmation, if not an answer. Why were they not coming forward or writing about it like their white counterparts?

In deciding exactly what it was that I wanted to share in this essay about my experiences with clinical depression, I realized that mental illness and race are topics that can not be divorced from one another. Not easily. Not for me. You see, the mask of depression is not all that different from the mask of race. So much of clinical depression has to do with identity, with images, with how those of us who suffer from the disease perceive ourselves and how, based on these oftentimes grossly distorted perceptions, we interact with others. So much of racism has to do with the same. It, too, barrages its prey with groundless images; it concerns itself more with the fiction of a prescribed identity than with the notion of any true individuality. It, too, seeks to blur a person's vision of herself, and her place in the world. Racism is also an illness. Perhaps not in the same way as depression, but an illness nonetheless. To contend with either one is bad enough. To grapple with both at the same time . . . that's enough to drive a person— pardon the expression—"crazy." Welcome to my insanity.

As a black woman struggling with depression, I don't know which I fear more: the identity of illness or the identity of wellness. One might imagine that the identity of wellness would, naturally, be the most desirable of the two. But that's usually the problem with desire: what you see is not necessarily what you get. The societal images of black female wellness, as evidenced (still) in present-day popular culture, have nothing at all to do with being well. Far from it. They have everything to do with the lies of history—a history that, invariably, has been shaped, created, or informed by the poisonous ideology of racism.

In these lies black women are strong. Strong enough to work two jobs while single-handedly raising twice as many children. Black women can cook, they can clean, they can sew, they can type, they can sweep, they can scrub, they can mop, and they can pray. Black women can—too. They are rarely romanticized, just oversexualized. Hookers, whores, Thursday-night concubines, and sultry-voiced back-alley blues club singers with Venus Hottentot hips. Either that or they are desexualized, just straight-up masculinized, mean-faced and hardened. Whatever the case, black women are always doing. They are always servicing everyone's needs, except their own. Their doing is what defines their being. And this is supposed to be wellness?

Not that the identity of illness is any better. Its only appeal is the allowance for vulnerability. You are able to need others, to invite their assistance, to accept their love—the catch is that you also have to be fragile. Anybody who's ever *really* been sick knows that the tolerance level for illness is low. Once the get-well roses begin to wilt, everything changes. Compassion and caretaking turn into burdens and vulnerability becomes weakness.

If the illness is something as nebulous as depression, folks begin to treat it like a character flaw: you are lazy, incapable, selfish, self-absorbed. The list is pretty much the same regardless of one's race. But race cannot and should not be disregarded; there is no room in the black female identity for weakness, laziness, incapability, selfishness, self-absorption, or even depression.

If I were to say that reading all the books by those depressed white people did not have a profound impact on my ability to come to terms with my own battle against depression, it would be disingenuous. Each one was like a mirror. Even if the external reflection looked nothing at all like me, what I saw of the internal reality was an accurate representation. The disease was the same, the symptoms were the same. The resulting confusion and hurt were the same.

None of that was enough though. I craved wholeness. I wanted to recognize *all* of me. Yet no matter how much these authors' confessions assuaged the discomfort I felt within, their stories could only meet the marrow and bone. They could never move outward and touch the flesh, the blackness that dictated the world in which I existed. What they could, and did, do was inspire me to write my own story. In writing that story I began, finally, to see why voices like mine were all but absent in discussions about depression. Let me show you what I mean:

Anecdote #1: While I was in the process of writing what would eventually become a memoir about my journey through depression, I was invited to a dinner party. It was a rather boring affair, the type that's full of old blue-haired women with fake teeth, fake fur, and real pearls. Not only was I one of the few people in the room under fifty, I was the only non-white person there as well. It wasn't my scene, so I didn't have much to offer by way of conversation, but the friend who brought me was, for some reason, determined to have me meet and make nice with the other guests, probably under the misguided assumption that they could help my career as an emerging writer. With great pride, he told one woman that I was writing a book.

The woman asked about the topic of my book. My friend took it upon himself to answer. "A book about black women and depression." The woman chuckled. "Black women and depression?" she asked. "Isn't that kinda redundant?" Everybody who heard this comment, including my friend, found humor in it. They laughed and laughed. Their obvious approval encouraged the woman. "Don't get me wrong," she continued. "It's just that when black women start going on Prozac, you know the whole world is falling apart."

Anecdote #2: Another dinner party. This time everyone in attendance was black and under forty. I was only casually acquainted with most of the people there. There were several clusters of conversation, including one being held by a group of women huddled in the kitchen. I joined them, figuring their conversation would be the most interesting. At parties, talk that takes place in the kitchen is usually simmering with colloquialism and candor. They were discussing pregnancy and childbirth. Two of the women were expecting, and everyone was taking turns telling tales of their own delivery dramas and dispensing wisdom that they'd heard or overheard from somebody who knew somebody who was an expert on these matters. Statements like, "Cocoa butter will make the stretch marks disappear," and, "They say that if you only breast-feed for three months, they won't sag after your milk is gone." Then someone other than me dropped the "d" word. "Hey, do you guys know anything about postpartum depression? I've been hearing about it a lot lately."

"Depression? I don't think they were talking about us. That is not a luxury we can afford."

"I'm telling you," another woman added. "That's all about white folks who don't have any real problems, so they have to create stuff to complain about. If black women started taking to their beds and crying about postpartum depression, who'd be left to play nanny to all those little white babies?"

Anecdote #3: When I was a creative-writing MFA [master of fine arts] student at Bennington College, I met Robert Bly, Mr. Iron John himself, the epitome of white male sensitivity. He was a guest faculty member. I was in the cafeteria searching for a place to park my tray when I noticed that Liam Rector, the director of the program, was having lunch with Bly. I decided to sit with them. I was introduced to Bly as a nonfiction student. He glanced in my direction and said hello. Then Liam added, "Meri is writing a book about black women and depression." Robert Bly looked over at me again and said, without hesitation, sarcasm, or irony, "Whew. That's going to be one really long book."

There is a lesson in each of these encounters, a soft sinew of truth connecting pain to power. It's always alarming to hear such opinions. They never fail to shock me, render me speechless. I don't believe that anyone actually thinks black women are, in some way, immune to clinical depression. I think it's simply that the black female identity of wellness—and all its silences—is ultimately preferable to the loud revelations that lie beyond the black female identity of wellness. After all, the women at both dinner parties were right. When black women fall apart, the world as we know it also falls apart. The myth of Mammy comes tumbling down.

Based on his frank reaction, Robert Bly obviously had some idea of what is hidden behind that myth. He was right when he suggested that the despair which generations of black women have had to endure could fill volumes. And, in fact, it has. From folklore to old wives' tales to contemporary novels, we have attempted to right the wrongs of our identity, to claim a humanity. Yet by and large, this documentation has been relegated to the pages of fiction. Which still positions our stories under the label of a lie, the invention of an artful imagination. Which prevents us from being able to distinguish diagnosable illnesses, like depression, from adaptive responses to the inequity of our circumstances, like despair. Which keeps us feeling fraudulent—as if we're not "keeping it real"—when we are not able to get out of bed on any given morning, let alone rise up to the challenge of life's hardships. What will it take to heal us of this legacy?

There is strength in numbers. It's hard to be the only one of anything—the only disabled student in a school, the only single mother in a community, the only immigrant on the job. You are perpetually aware of your difference. After I met two other black women who were willing to openly admit that they were also dealing with depression, the sense of helplessness I had been feeling when I thought I was all alone turned into a sense of hopefulness. They were walking, talking, breathing people—not well-crafted characters. Their experiences authenticated mine in a way that nothing else could. Their presence addressed all of the questions and issues I had about what it means to be a black woman living with a psychological disorder. It means seeing yourself in a way that is often inconsistent with the way the world sees you. It means seeing yourself as a human being who is entitled to a wide range of human emotions and conditions, including illness and wellness.

By the time my memoir, *Willow Weep for Me*, was published, I had undergone various methods of treatment for my depression. Therapy, antidepressants, mood stabilizers—some of which were ineffective and others of which worked marvelously. I had become unashamed of the illness and unafraid of its stigma. Moreover, I had moved past the tendency to view my life against the blinding background of whiteness, the need to paint it with predetermined images of blackness. Every now and then, I find myself thinking about those white Jewish women from Boston. I find myself wondering about their reaction to *my* story. Do they read my work and see more than race? Can they enter my world and recognize something of themselves in my reflection?

SOCIAL ISSUES
FIRSTHAND

CHAPTER 3

Getting Help

Learning to Accept Help

Art Greco

Diagnosed with "stress-induced depression," Art Greco decided to hide his illness from everyone except his doctor and to handle his depression alone. As a church pastor, he felt that if anyone, including his family, knew about his illness, it would be considered a sign of weakness. However, changes in his behavior became apparent to his wife and to a number of leaders in his church, and they began to question him. Eventually admitting to his diagnosis, Greco received support from those around him and took a paid leave of absence from his job to obtain treatment.

In this article Greco lists some of the lessons he learned during his struggle with depression. He learned that accepting help was an essential part of his healing process, and that although the Bible and his spiritual life were important to him, working with a skilled therapist was also necessary. He also talks about how his painful and difficult experience helped him to grow, as a person and as a pastor.

A s my blue Mazda 626 rolled to a stop at the light, I had no idea my life would take an immediate turn. I was thinking only of getting home to watch the Cubs on cable while I ate my lunch.

The corner of Highway 99 and McDonald Street has one of those lights that always seems to be red—especially when I'm on my way home. On the left was Elmer's Restaurant, the "after worship" eatery for many families in our church, and on the right was Union Gas Station. Everything looked familiar.

I felt normal, meaning stressed. I assumed the tightness in my chest and pressure in my head (but without the sharp

Art Greco, "Attacked by a Monster: Depression Hit Me by Surprise, and Help Came Despite My Foolish Reactions," *Leadership*, Spring 2005, pp. 76–80. Reproduced by permission of the author.

pain of a headache) was the expected byproduct of being a church planter. I was a little dizzy—all things I had grown accustomed to.

Suddenly something bizarre happened. Nothing looked familiar. It was like that feeling you get when, in the middle of the night, exhausted during a road trip, you awaken in a half conscious, panicked fog. Your surroundings are strange and you can't remember where you are—until you realize you're in a hotel room, not in your bed back home. Only in this case, clarity wasn't returning. I didn't know where I was, where I was going, or where I'd been. I just sat there, dazed, until the car behind me honked and startled me into creeping through a now foreign light that had turned green.

I motored slowly down the highway, thinking, *I'll just keep driving until something looks familiar.* I turned left because it "felt" correct, then left again for the same reason. *I think I live on this block.* But I wasn't sure which house was mine.

Push the button on the garage door opener, I thought. *Wherever a garage door opens, that must be my house.* When I noticed a garage opening, I parked in the driveway, walked into the garage, and sat on the freezer, waiting for my head to clear. I wondered if my ministry was over because of some serious and debilitating disease.

That happened in the spring of 1991, and it started a chain of struggles, errors, and lessons that have proven to be among the most significant in my life.

One of those errors happened right there in the garage. As I sat groping and pleading with God for mental clarity, my son came home from school. "What's wrong, Dad?" he asked. "Why aren't you at work?"

Keeping Depression to Himself

I decided to keep this experience to myself. How could the family handle having a dad who couldn't find his way home for lunch? I would see my doctor because I wanted to know what the problem was. But I determined to deal with this thing alone.

After several medical tests, the doctor's diagnosis was "stress-induced depression," and he recommended that I find another profession. This, too, I kept to myself. Not even my wife knew. While my motivation was to protect her, it was a foolish, unloving, even dangerous decision.

That was the first of many bad decisions. What follows is an abbreviated list of the lessons learned in my ongoing struggle with this monster called depression.

Don't Try to Handle It Alone

1. Trying to handle depression alone is its own type of insanity. I eventually learned that recovering from depression requires help from other people. In fact, my martyr-like approach, had I stayed with it, could have been disastrous.

I was afraid that people would see me as weak, that the stresses of planting a church and functioning as pastor were too much for me. I wasn't going to tell the church's leadership; I wasn't going to tell my wife; and I *sure* wasn't going to tell my superintendent. Pride convinced me that I would be branded it anyone found out. But, thankfully, keeping my secret eventually turned out to be impossible.

Despite my silence, Brenda knew something was wrong. There were evenings when I would come home from work and go to bed. I didn't want to talk, I was irritable, and I began to isolate myself.

One night Brenda told me that a member of the church was on the phone with a question about a minor ministry detail. I refused to take the call. Throwing up my arms and retreating to the bedroom, I screamed, "Why do people always call *me*? Why can't they just leave me alone? When do *I* get a life?"

My church leaders and close friends were also too bright for my cover-up. I fooled them for a while, but soon I was "blanking" during sermons and depending entirely on my notes, something I hated.

In addition, I began to forget the names of folks I'd known for years. I was short with people at business meetings, when before I had been playful.

I would do anything to avoid a "get together" or follow up on a guest to our church. My close associates didn't say much at first. But eventually they began to ask probing questions. Realizing that I was not getting better, I finally confided in our church chairperson, one of my closest friends, and explained what was happening.

He wisely insisted that I tell my wife, that the leaders be informed, that the church pay for a second opinion (which eventually confirmed the original diagnosis), and that he and I sit down with our superintendent to ask for help.

Letting others help was pivotal in my healing. To my surprise, most people actually felt closer to me, even energized by the opportunity to help their pastor. While this, I suspect, would not be the case in every congregation, I am confident that many pastors struggling with stress, depression, or burnout would be encouraged by their church's ability and desire to help.

Accept Help

2. A pastor does no one any favors by refusing to accept help. Our leadership was sensitive and understanding. They talked with the doctor they had sent me to and decided to give me six months off (with full pay and a good therapeutic strategy) to recuperate. I was ready to accept their offer, but not without first negotiating it down a bit. Six months away was just too much.

This seemingly "noble" decision to reduce the offered time off was another mistake. I told myself that so much paid time off was unfair to an already struggling church. But really, my primary discomfort was driven by pride. There I was, a man who could hardly make it through a day without going home to hide in his bedroom, too proud to accept the very gift that was the recommended route to recovery.

At my insistence, we settled on a month off, after which I'd work 20 hours per week, finally easing back to full time over the span of two to three months. My leaders and my physician all argued for the original six months, but true to prideful form, I held firm. Now I realize I was wrong and regret the decision. It would have been better for them and me if I had humbly accepted their gift of love.

During that month away, I was able to focus on some of the unbiblical views I had formed about success. I considered their role in my struggle. I experienced wonderful talks with God as I worked in my garden and even took a full week alone to just drive south and be completely spontaneous as the Lord led me along.

I made so much progress—laughing again, sensing hope and value, experiencing occasional peace and the virtual absence of stress—that I was convinced I should get back to work as soon as the month was up.

But thinking you can go back to ministry "part time" when you've been a full-time pastor for so long is pretty unreasonable. It wasn't long before I found myself working six days and most evenings, and slipping back into the dark hole that had previously consumed me.

Once again, I began closing my blinds and locking my office door just in case someone decided to come for a visit or prayer, letting the answering machine take calls I would have otherwise picked up myself. I was retreating again. And fearing that a full-blown depression was returning.

Partly because I was learning to talk about my struggles and partly because I was being assisted by new medications, these "signs that I hadn't yet recovered" did not lead to another complete breakdown. But I clearly returned to ministry too soon and my recovery was much more painful than it needed to be.

Get Help in Addition to the Bible

3. Assuming that all I need is the Bible is tempting but dangerous. Some pastors resist receiving help that isn't exclusively theological or scriptural in approach. Others are so used to being the ones giving help that they find it difficult to receive any. And of course, some question the ministry of Christian therapy altogether. I was a member of the second and third groups.

"The Scriptures are my therapist," I would say, "and they don't charge me $100 per hour."

Certainly the Bible contributed much to my recovery. Its comforts were amazing, its instructions and insights incredible. But being forced by my circumstances to ask for help from an able counselor changed my entire outlook. Without that wonderful man's prayer, honest questioning, and practical help, I don't know how long it would have taken me to heal, or if I ever *would* have.

I continue to find strength and guidance from the Word of God. But in it I read about the importance of Christian community in discerning the deep things of the Spirit. In my experience, it was the Bible in partnership with a gifted, discerning therapist that God used to loose me from the hands of this unrelenting monster.

Get Through the Day

4. Sometimes the objective isn't defeating the depression but simply getting through today for the opportunity to take another step tomorrow. At times, the depression was so strong that I could not imagine that it could ever be defeated. The thought that I would have to live with its poisonous suffocation for the next 20 years only added to its strength over me. Even before I knew that it was a good tactic, I was practicing the discipline of being concerned only for the day I was actually *in*, not worrying about how dark the days to follow might be.

The script played out as follows: Mornings usually served to remind me that nothing had really changed. I was still choking emotionally and my soul still couldn't breathe. Often I fantasized about how nice it would have been to die. I would need to consider three reasons to stay alive today.

So I would think about the three children I love so much, and the scars they would carry the rest of their lives if I ended mine. Reason number two might be my parents. Wouldn't they be haunted by guilt, wondering what they could have done differently or, worse, whether they might have contributed to the depression in some way? They didn't deserve that.

Most powerfully, I would think of my wife. How could I possibly consider suicide a fair payment for the sweet, selfless loyalty she had offered me all these years?

On other days I would consider different reasons, like the kids in our church who'd question the validity of faith in Christ every time they remembered their pastor who committed suicide. Sometimes those "reasons" were as superficial as wanting to watch the Dodgers game that weekend or that I still hadn't finished the lasagna in the fridge (and Brenda makes great lasagna).

It was too big a leap to think about defeating depression in one stroke. That kind of thinking only tightened its hopeless grip on me. No, my objective was just to get through the day, telling myself, "Tomorrow might be better, and I will never know unless I make sure it is available to me."

At times, I would literally recite: "My objective today is just to stay alive in order to have another chance to chip away at it tomorrow."

Learn from Your Experience

5. Depression can be a great teacher. Anyone reading this article while struggling with these things is probably ready to tear it out and toss it right about now. I certainly would have those 14 years ago.

I can't forget the well-meaning but exquisitely painful platitudes offered by others during those days of depression. The most well-rehearsed was, "Well, God must love you very much and want to do something wonderful in your life to allow you to go through all of this."

It was true, of course, that God loved me. And he had at least *allowed* what I was experiencing. But those platitudes always hurt more than they helped. In fact, they *never* helped! So I apologize to anyone who is shaken by the assertion that God might want to use things as painful as depression to do good, or that depression can be a "companion" that enriches or helps us in any way.

But, speaking from the other side of the despair, yet aware that another episode could be right around the corner, I can say that God *did* do good things through this "uninvited friend."

Parts of me died through that trial—parts of me that I really liked. For instance, I am off the charts in my "E" (extrovert) score on the Myers Briggs test. Previously, I could never get enough of people. Even on our honeymoon I said to my new bride, "Okay, it's been great to be alone for a couple of days. Now what do you say we go home early, get a bunch of friends together, and have a party?" (By the way, I recommend that you *not* say this on your honeymoon—or on any romantic excursion.)

During my struggle with depression, I found that I didn't want to be with folks much, if at all. The thought of answering the phone or entertaining a group brought on a "headache in my chest." Even now, I tend to go home before everyone else has left an event. I now consider it as something precious to be alone and quiet for extended periods of time. I still love gatherings and thrive on encounters, but not as much as I used to. Part of that died, and part of it *needed* to.

But there are new things that God birthed in me as a direct result of this nightmare too. I was humbled by my neediness and my inability to subdue that depression monster. However, the embarrassment and subsequent humiliation made me much more approachable to people.

One neighbor who had recently begun to follow Christ said to me after my return to work, "I've noticed that something has changed in you. You're not nearly so threatening as you used to be. I think I'm ready to get involved in your church now."

A Curse and a Grace

A friend of mine, quoting an African American pastor, once said, "If you ain't got no need, your prayers ain't got no suction." I wish I could say that I no longer experience bouts with depression. I can't say that. But I *can* say that the monster doesn't roam the halls of my life with the lordship it once did.

I *can* say that I've learned that there's calm on the other side of those bouts, that I'm no longer as afraid of them.

And I can *definitely* say that depression has often been the only thing that could pin my nose to the carpet before the Lord's feet. In reminding me of my need, it gives my prayers suction.

I would never want to go through that experience again. It was as close to hell as I would ever care to wander. Yet this misery has proven to be so strategic in my life as a Christian and a pastor that I would never want to erase it from my history either. So much pain was experienced in the heat of that fire, but still, so much good has been found in the stain of its ashes.

What a mystery—to have something serve as curse and grace, at the same time.

Being with Others Who Understand

Sharon O'Brien

Sharon O'Brien, an author and professor of literature, was nervous about attending her first Manic-Depressive and Depressive Association (MDDA) meeting. She quickly realized, however, that being part of a group of people suffering from an illness similar to hers can be exhilarating. In her professional life, she is known by her accomplishments. In this group, she can speak of her sufferings and struggles.

In this article O'Brien talks about the structure of MDDA group meetings and how the group functions. She describes how members support one another by sharing their stories, speaking honestly with one another, and expressing gratitude for positive signs, no matter how small. The group helps her to focus not on looking for a happy ending and a complete recovery, but rather on learning to live with a chronic illness.

I'm driving through Belmont [Massachusetts], on my way to McLean's Hospital and my first meeting of MDDA, the Manic-Depressive and Depressive Association. It's an advocacy and support group, the local chapter of a national organization. I've known of its existence for a few months but haven't been ready to go. Attending this group has represented defeat, a sign that depression would be a permanent part of my life instead of a mind storm just passing through. Surely the people who attend are much sicker than *me*: as long as I don't go, I can maintain my separateness, and the story that I will, some day, recover.

But I'm still stuck in my midwinter doldrums and desperate for change. Tonight I walked home from Harvard Square in the five o'clock dark of mid-December, threw down my backpack, fed the cat, and sat on the couch for an hour, watching *Frasier* reruns I'd seen twice before. I knew the MDDA meeting was at 7:30. At least it would pass the time.

Nervous About Her First Meeting

I drive up Belmont Street, past the funeral home where my parents were waked, past Lewis Road, our old street, past Our Lady of Mercy Church, the site of my first communion and my parents' funeral masses. On the left is one of the few remaining Brigham's, the ice cream store where my father would stop in for his coffee milkshake, and where I lurked on Sundays during college, too afraid to tell my parents I was no longer going to Mass. At Waverley Square I take the right fork—the left fork would take me to the small apartment my mother moved to after my father died, the apartment where she herself died, in her own bed, all three of us there, the way she wanted. I drive past the Duck Pond and past all the long-ago Thanksgivings, the mornings when my father took me and my brother to feed the ducks so my mother could have "room to breathe." Then the right turn into McLean's.

McLean's is a famous, and privileged, mental hospital associated with Harvard University. When I was in high school, kids went there to park; undisturbed back lanes would be dotted with parents' cars and entwined couples on Saturday nights after a dance. McLean's is also the celebrated place of incarceration for writers I've taught—Robert Lowell, Sylvia Plath, Susanna Kaysen. I've been here once before: a visit to a psychiatrist more than twenty years ago, the summer my father lay voiceless and dying in the intensive care unit at Mass General. I must have had to tell somebody what it was like to not be able to tell the truth to your dying father who could no longer speak or write. So I drove up to a mental hospital and told the truth to a stranger. "Families only become more themselves during a crisis," the psychiatrist said.

I feel nervous going to McLean's. This venture brings out my native shyness: walking into this unknown group makes me feel like a kid starting camp in the middle of the month, knowing all the experienced campers have been there for two weeks. I'm somewhat reassured by a check-in line for nametags: at least I don't have to walk, all unprotected, into a horde of strangers who know each other. As I write my name on a red-bordered tag (blue is for regulars) and look around a cafeteria filled with more than a hundred nametagged people I have a strange sensation. I scan some of the nametags near me—Mary Ellen, Robert, David, Barbara, Karen—and think *All of these people suffer from depression or manic-depression, and they don't look any different from anybody else, any different from me.* Of course I've known this in my head, but somehow seeing so many people in the same room—it could be any group—announcing by their presence and their names that they have—well, *suffered*—is oddly exhilarating.

Her First Meeting

After I sign my nametag (just "Sharon," no last names or professional affiliations here), the woman in charge advises me to attend the Newcomers group. I join the other red-nametagged people while the older blue-tagged campers go off to their own discussion groups. An old-timer named Charlie is our discussion leader. He gives us the MDDA rules: our discussions are confidential, no outside observers unless everyone in the group agrees, give support but not advice. He introduces himself by telling his own depression story. "I'm sixty-six years old and I think I've been depressed since I was four. I've lost more jobs than you can count and spent more years than you'd like to think looking into a bottle. Now I'm not doing so bad, on a new medication, sometimes the docs can't keep up with me, and thanks of course to this group." He pauses and nods to the man next to him, who's wearing stained carpenter's pants and staring straight ahead. The nod is a sign that he should introduce himself, but the man keeps staring and finally Charlie picks somebody else to go first.

It is unexpectedly moving just to listen to the check-ins and introductions. "I'm John, I've been struggling with depression for twenty years." John is dysthymic and hasn't found a medication that works. "I'm Stuart," says a man gripping the seat of his chair. "I'm in McLean's right now. I'm pretty suicidal, I guess. Lithium isn't working and they haven't been able to find meds that work." Stuart doesn't speak during group: he's barely hanging in, trying to make it until 9:00 P.M. and his sleeping medication. "I'm Anne," a woman says. "I'm still working on trying to regain custody," and people nod sympathetically. "I've been out of the hospital about three weeks now, no panic attacks, so I can be grateful for that." I will later realize such comments are typical; people in MDDA are always finding what they can be grateful for. "The rapid cycling is pretty bad right now, but I'm in the day program here and I think it's helping." "I've been pretty down for the last few weeks"—here "pretty down" doesn't mean "somewhat dispirited," it means "practically leveled"—"but I'm still able to go to work, so that's good."

When professional colleagues introduce me at talks and conferences, they list my accomplishments and honors and merit badges. Here everything is reversed as I introduce myself by what is silenced out there. "I'm Sharon, and I've suffered from major depression on and off since I was a teenager, pretty intensely for the last ten years. I've tried almost fifteen antidepressants but nothing's really worked yet." People look at me, one or two gasp in sympathy, everyone's faces are welcoming and I have an unfamiliar feeling of belonging. They understand what's below the surface of those few words, just as I understand the unspoken months and years of suffering when they speak. When we use the word "depressed" we all know we're not talking about the ordinary lows that everyone experiences, we're not talking about feeling down. We have a common language, and we know we're talking about the untranslatable depths. "I'm not doing too well right now," I add, and people nod again.

They know what "not too well" means.

As I say the words "I'm Sharon" to a group of strangers, I know I'm doing something that some people, including many of my academic colleagues, would satirize. Support groups are easy targets for people who find the verb "share" humorous, I've heard the phrase "Thank you for sharing" used ironically hundreds of times; I've read Wendy Kaminer's witty, detached debunking of the recent epidemic of "codependency" and "recovery" groups; I've listened to many jokes beginning with "I'm [name]" that mock the classic support group introduction, and in the past I've probably laughed at them. Maybe right now I'm doing something that other academics would find self-indulgent or laughable or politically retrograde.

I have to say, I really don't care.

After me it's the staring man's turn. "I'm Don," he says in a flattened voice, his eyes dull chips of coal. "I'm bipolar, been in and out of hospitals maybe twenty times. I don't hold out much hope for getting better but I thought I'd try this group." He is wearing a long-sleeved jersey, but it's shrunk from many washings. His wrists are ropy with scars.

"We're glad you came, Don," Charlie says. Don doesn't look at him. He leaves during the break.

Driving home, I feel like I'm a new recruit in a war that's been going on a long time. I'm going to go back and get my blue nametag.

Knowing the Routine

It doesn't take long before I get to know the MDDA routine. Every other week we listen to a talk before we have groups— topics like "Health Care Parity," "Dual Diagnosis in Children," "Electroshock Therapy," "Side Effects." The speaker stands behind a podium that carries the MDDA logo—the words

"Unipolar/Bipolar" and two polar bears, one seated and shivering, paws over its eyes, the other cockily prancing in the sun, waving a walking stick, about to burst into a soft-shoe routine. When the question period is over an MDDA officer comes to the podium to announce where the support groups are meeting. "Okay," he says, "tonight it's Newcomers in 112, Friends and Family in 113, Employment in 114, Women's in 115, Wellness in 116, Manics in 117—don't make too much noise, you guys—and depressives, you're in the lounge outside." He pauses. "We all know *you'll* be quiet."

At first I thought the list was just plain funny, but come to appreciate and respect the straightforward room assignments, the willingness, which I find everywhere in MDDA, to avoid euphemisms. People don't stumble and trip or lower their voices when they say words like "manic," "depression," "suicide," "hospitalization," the way they often do in the outside world.

Some of us shift around among the groups, depending on our moods and needs. It might be Employment for two weeks, then Women's, then back to Employment and on to Depressives. Officially we're not supposed to go to Friends and Family just to find out what they think about us: you're required to have friends or family with mood disorders to attend this group, but most of us do so the point is moot. Other people pick one group as home base.

At first I attend Depressives but after a few weeks I switch to Wellness. I'd been resisting because I hate the word "wellness," but I'd gotten to know the facilitator and he invited me to sit in. My depression was lifting a little and I wanted to start focusing more on prevention and coping. Besides, all the bipolars in Wellness gave the group a lot more energy.

Most people in Wellness were suffering from chronic mood disorders and were working on managing them. They were all acquainted with grief but weren't giving up, so there was an atmosphere in the room of, if not hope, at least stubborn persistence, and sometimes a cathartic black humor.

"I'm sorry for interrupting during check-ins again," says Bill, a bipolar who's in the day program at MGH [Massachusetts General Hospital]. "I know that's one of the things I need to work on."

"And as we know, that's the least of your problems," observes the facilitator, who's shared hospital time with Bill.

The check-ins continue. "I think I've been depressed all my life." "I was diagnosed manic six months ago and I think I'm still adjusting." "I'm feeling normal for the first time in years, and it's great, but I keep looking over my shoulder. I don't trust it." "I'm just recovering from a manic episode and I'm feeling so bad about all the stupid and hurtful things I did when I was high." People nod. We all *get* it in our bones, no matter where we are on the spectrum right now, whether we're high functioners like the facilitator—"high functioner" is MDDA lingo for somebody who's either in a good space or whose illness isn't too bad—or working every minute just to stay alive.

Nobody's passing here.

Lightening the Sadness with Humor

At the break I'm startled to hear people make mood disorder jokes. "How many ECTs does it take to screw in a light bulb?" asks Don, the group leader.

I haven't heard the abbreviation before, but I catch on: ECTs must be people who've had electroshock treatments.

"I don't know. How many?"

"I forget." Everybody laughs.

"I don't get it," I whisper to Charlie. "Memory loss, a side effect," he whispers back.

"How many depressives does it take?" Don asks.

"I give up," everybody says, playing the game.

"None. They haven't noticed that the light has gone out."

People say things casually to each other they'd find insulting in the outside world. Here it's a form of teasing. Phil, an earnest depressive who's intrigued by the diagnostic codes of the DSM [*Diagnostic and Statistical Manual of Mental Disorders*] wants to know if it's true that only one manic episode can qualify you as bipolar.

"In your *dreams*, Phil," says Marybeth, who's bipolar. "What are you, a wannabe?"

People can make the kind of demeaning remarks about the mentally ill they would never, in these politically correct days, make about blacks and gays. Making jokes is a way to take our power of naming back from the culture. It's also a way of reinforcing our momentary "outness." All of us possess many identities—we're bipolar or unipolar, yes, and we can also be teachers, social workers, parents, cooks, wine-lovers, Italian and Irish and WASP [white, Anglo-Saxon Protestants], Little League coaches, journal keepers, Buddhists, soccer players, poets, aunts, madrigal singers, gardeners, and citizens. The only thing is, none of those other identities are deviant. So when we play with the language the medical profession uses to define us it's a way to resist the stigma.

We can tease each other because, in an odd way, we're family. I've never known anyone who was manic-depressive until I got involved with MDDA, and now it seems that we unipolars and bipolars are first cousins.

There's a place for humor because there's so much sadness to be borne. During the year a woman from Wellness, one of the sparkplugs, commits suicide. None of us can believe it. We all can believe it.

Being a Regular Part of the Group

I stay with the group for the rest of my year in Boston, soon finding myself one of the "regulars" in the Wellness group. A ritual develops—organized by one of the bipolars—of adjourning to the Ground Round, a local restaurant, after the meeting, for snacks, conversation, and drinks—usually coke, sprite, or coffee, since people are either in recovery or taking meds that don't mix with alcohol. Under normal circumstances I'll allow myself a glass of wine, but during my year in Boston I give up alcohol entirely—it's a depressant—and join the decaf coffee drinkers.

I come to look forward to my Wednesday nights. For me, attending this group—and so admitting openly to depression—is about accepting the ongoing reality of the illness. And accepting depression, as I finally will understand, is a process, not an action. The more times I attend this group, the more times I name myself as a sufferer from depression, the more times I go to the Ground Round and tease the bipolars ("Thank *God* for your energy, without you we depressives would just creep right home to bed"), the more times I fight denial. If I gave denial a chance, I'd be checking the news for the latest wonder drug, the newly unveiled antidepressant that, this time, is going to work for sure.

I make friends with Annette, diagnosed with manic depression a few years ago. She's got one of the best reasons for coming to MDDA. "If I'm hospitalized again," she says, "I want lots of people to visit me. I mean *lots*." Annette's first (and so far only) hospitalization was very successful. She wants to be sure that any subsequent ones measure up. "I didn't even know there was a stigma about manic depression," she says. "I was in my twenties, a complete innocent. Didn't know there was anything wrong with being bipolar till later, when everyone was telling me how brave I was to be so up front."

When she was hospitalized Annette called everybody she could think of to tell them, family, friends, faculty at her graduate school. "I had fourteen people visiting me the first night—most people didn't have anybody—and they could hardly fit into my room. Balloons, candy, flowers, the works. It was worth it."

I like the image: lots of cheery, gift-laden visitors crowding their way onto a locked ward. "If I'm ever hospitalized that's what I want too," I say. It's a revolutionary idea. I've always feared hospitalization for depression. I've imagined being in some back ward, trapped, desperate, forgotten, and alone. I never thought about visiting hours. I'd probably be taken to Hershey Medical Center, thirty miles away—but there's no reason why my friends can't make the drive, bringing me *People* magazine and the Sunday *Times* and cafe lattes. Balloons, too. When you read *One Flew over the Cuckoo's Nest* or *Girl, Interrupted* it never occurs to you that if you were in a mental hospital your friends could bring you balloons and good coffee.

"If I'm hospitalized I definitely want balloons," I tell her.

"I tied mine to the bars in the window and they lasted for two days," Annette says. "If I have to go to McLean's, I want everybody in the group to know, everybody to visit. I'm committed, I'm networking."

No Happy Endings

I like going to the meetings because I know I don't have to be upbeat, the way I am sometimes with friends whose patience I fear is running thin. Maybe I've asked for too much, maybe I haven't given enough back; you start thinking in terms of emotional economy when you have a chronic illness. Have you invested enough to be able to make a withdrawal? Have you overdrawn your friendship account? Sometimes your well-intentioned friends who've never been depressed say "It's going to be okay, don't worry," not knowing—how could they?—that sometimes that feels like a dismissal. "Sometimes I just get sick of people telling me 'it will be all right,'" a man says at a group meeting. "I mean, I'm not going to give up, at least I don't think so, but things are never really going to be all right." Strange as it may seem, sometimes that's just what you want to hear, someone else saying that things are not ever, really, going to be all right. Because as long as you feel there's a happy ending up ahead you're not reaching, you cannot be content with your life.

People at MDDA, I notice, never tell each other that everything is going to be all right. They listen to your story and give you understanding, and they tell theirs and you give understanding back. After meetings they say "See you next week," and "Are you going to the picnic?" and "Hang in there" and "Call me if you need to."

Good Days Are a Gift

"So do you think there's such a thing as recovery?" a man in my depression support group asks. "A permanent breakthrough?"

No one speaks for a while, and then a woman who's bipolar—"not doing too bad this week"—says "even if I felt good for a long time, I mean a *long* time, I wouldn't trust it. I'd be waiting for the other shoe to drop," and several people nod. "Waiting for the other shoe to drop" is a phrase that recurs often in my group when people go through stable periods. Another is "looking over my shoulder," as when someone says, "I've been feeling quite good lately, for a few months now, but I keep looking over my shoulder," laughing apologetically, "wondering what's gaining on me."

"So how do you feel when you have good days?" someone asks the bipolar woman.

"Like they're a gift," she says, and people murmur assent.

Like most of the people who attend my support group, I'm not just learning how to manage a chronic illness. I'm working on finding a new story for my life, a story that gives me hope but doesn't require the happy ending of recovery. This is a struggle in America, a culture that celebrates and practically requires individual achievement, a culture where we don't have enough stories for imagining lives that do not fit, in one way or another, the success plot.

Adjusting Medications Is Complex

David A. Karp

In preparation for his book Is it Me or My Meds? *David A. Karp, who suffers from depression himself, interviewed people about their experiences with antidepressant drugs. In the following excerpt Karp interviews "Mike," a man with manic-depressive illness. Mike was initially placed on a drug called amitriptyline, and in two weeks he felt like a new person. After about a year of treatment, the drug stopped working. Karp describes Mike's numerous unsuccessful attempts at finding another drug that would work as well, coming to the conclusion that while antidepressants "work" for some people, for many more they only provide partial relief or sometimes no relief at all.*

Mike is an energetic, physically fit man who in his twenties sparred regularly with a regional welterweight champion. I was eager to interview Mike, whose work as a depression support group facilitator I had long admired. Mike often described himself in group meetings as "treatment resistant," so I was especially interested in documenting his thoughts on drugs and illness. When I thanked him for putting aside an evening to talk to me, he explained that mornings were not an option for him, since he suffered from "poverty of thought" until well into the afternoon: "You'd think [in the morning] that I never read anything [and] hadn't been on the planet for the last fifty years, because there's just nothing that can be retrieved. It's horrible."

Although he described the adolescent rebellion of his teenage years as including all-weekend partying, heavy drinking, and a relationship with his father characterized by "pushing each other's buttons," he did well in his small-town prep school, and was even elected class president. As a high school student, he could not have recognized that having "more energy than I knew what to do with and [getting] really wound up at times" were symptoms of mild hypomania (a stage of mania during which individuals entertain grand ideas, are filled with energy, can get along without much sleep, feel extremely creative, and can accomplish an enormous amount of work—a stage that often precedes an episode of psychotic mania). In fact, he was not diagnosed with bipolar illness until his early thirties. Even without a diagnosis, though, he knew by the time he entered college that something was wrong. As a freshman premed major he "got hit with depression and . . . could go to the library for six hours and nothing would sink in." "I did that for a semester," he told me, "and was really messed up and just withdrawn." He did have a capacity for cramming—later seen as connected to hypomania—that sometimes kept him awake for long periods. Indeed, he discovered that "if you stay up long enough the depression will lift. . . . You can go from suicidal, to twenty-four hours without sleep, to being very social, outgoing, and optimistic about life."

Like so many who go for years suffering from an undiagnosed illness, Mike medicated himself. In his case it was with "grass every night before I went to bed," hashish, alcohol, and occasionally amphetamines. The "edge of craziness" he experienced during those years made it impossible to relax without recreational drugs or strenuous physical activity. His taste for danger as a way of combating anxiety led him to downhill skiing "because of the intensity of the speed" and to boxing with the welterweight, who "beat me up four times a week." None of these activities dulled his emotional pain, and he soon left school for a job as a long-distance trucker. The job provided some relief: "When I was out of town and on the road . . . I didn't have anybody telling me what to do." Mike eventually returned to school, went through an "ugly divorce," and entered Alcoholics Anonymous in the belief that his problems were the result of alcohol abuse. Although he stopped drinking, his depression and anxiety persisted, and at age thirty-four, Mike had to face the possibility that there was something deeply wrong with *him.*

While he initially resisted seeing a psychiatrist because he "felt it was humiliating" and "didn't want anybody telling me there was anything wrong with my head," the depression and the desperation it created eventually pushed him into a doctor's office. When I asked Mike if he was also initially resistant to medications, he replied:

> No, I was in so much pain that I really didn't care what I had to take to get out of the pain. When the depression got really bad, I knew that I was drinking to deal with the depression, and I knew that drinking relieved the depression. So . . . I was tuned into the fact that you could do something chemically and relieve the depression. So . . . for me there wasn't any resistance at all.

It is one of the ironies of Mike's long history with medications that only the very first drug he took gave him sustained relief. At that time the drugs most commonly prescribed for depression belonged to a class known as tricyclic antidepressants, one of the earliest of which was amitriptyline: "[My doctor] gave me amitriptyline, which is . . . supposed to take two . . . to six weeks to work. It took two weeks. I felt like a brand-new person. . . . I was amazed." No doubt Mike's later disappointments with a wide array of drugs were deepened by their contrast with this early success. Buoyed by good health and the discovery that he had a natural talent for carpentry, he enthusiastically made plans for a new career. However, "Just about a year to the day, the stuff stopped working." At that point the depression was only momentarily relieved by periods of hypomania:

Then I started into this pattern of two and a half to three weeks of . . . mild hypomania where I felt really good and was focused and could function. Then I would start going downhill. . . . I was exercising again through all of this. . . . When I started going downhill, I would start intensifying the amount of exercise I did, thinking that . . . I was going back to that runner's high . . . I used to be able to get. But no matter what I did . . . if the depression started on a Sunday, no matter how hard I tried, by Wednesday I would be lying on the bed, curled up and aching . . . in a state of absolute despair and physically aching. And . . . I was saying to myself, "Depression can't make you ache because it's just in my mind. I'm depressed in my head, so how can I be aching from this?" I would be at the point where I would be so depressed I'd just give up. And then I wouldn't even try and help myself. . . . I'd reached the point where [I was] lying in bed on . . . Wednesday . . . Thursday, possibly Friday, and then, without any effort, I would just come right up out of the depression. And I didn't realize that I was mildly hypomanic at the time.

When, years previously, Mike had returned to an undergraduate program following his truck-driving stint, he had majored in psychology. I asked what he felt about biological and psychological explanations for mental illness. Recalling his success with amitriptyline, he replied with some animation:

I just get really . . . pissed off about all the psychological theories that I've read. . . . When I went back to [college] . . . I was able to go through those [psychological] theories . . . from all different angles to try and understand just what was causing [my] level of depression. Then, after two weeks [on amitriptyline], I said, "Oh man, this [psychology stuff] is just . . . bullshit."

Despite the eventual failure of the medication, Mike's taste of drug success solidified his commitment to a biomedical view of his illness. His experience was profound enough to foster his belief in what the sociologist Allan Horwitz has called "diagnostic psychiatry," with its unflinching commitment to bio-chemical solutions. Such a belief system is nearly always the backdrop for years of experimentation with a series of medications.

It is hard to overstate the difficulty of starting a new drug, staying on it for enough time to determine its effects, adjusting doses to minimize side effects, and then weaning yourself off when it doesn't work. In the 1970s Mike quickly worked his way through a series of tricyclics, including nortriptyline, imipramine, and desipramine. He also tried lithium, a natural salt, which was "a major negative event. . . . It just knocked me on my ass." At some point during this period Mike also tried, without success, another category of antidepressants called MAOIs (monoamine oxidase inhibitors), which can cause dangerous reactions, even death, if mixed with certain foods.

Since Mike's doctor believed in giving each medication at least a six-week trial before discarding it, you can imagine how long Mike spent on this exhausting drug merry-go-round. He did the math for me: "If we went through five drugs that didn't work, that could be thirty or forty weeks of drug trials and nothing is working. But when we left them behind we left them behind. . . . If we revisited them it was only in desperation." Then, with the arrival of the SSRIs [selective serotonin reuptake inhibitors, a group of drugs prescribed for depression and anxiety] in the early 1980s, he began another round of experiments, one drug at a time:

> I started going around in a circle again. . . . The SSRIs had come in. Well, the SSRIs were a complete waste. One after another made me sick. Prozac when it first came out was the miracle drug, so . . . I was willing to put up with feeling like nauseated to the point of just about throwing up for about two weeks and staying sick in bed trying to adjust to the Prozac. [I was] thinking, "Well, what's the alternative? Nothing's working. And this is the drug that's taking people off the back wards." So, you know, it's a reason to hang in

there with this. That's how Prozac affected me. . . . Finally after two weeks I stopped taking it. Then I think . . . I started working my way through the SSRIs . . . and they're not working, one after another. Then I get into Paxil. Paxil has me nauseated. . . . I stayed on it for a while . . . trying to adjust to it because of what it did. The first eight hours after I take a Paxil I am sick, really sick. The second eight hours . . . I'm sick and shaky. . . . Then after eight hours of being sick and shaky I start getting a little bit of relief. . . . So I figure, "Okay, maybe I'm going to adjust to this." So I tried this for, you know, a few weeks, but . . . sick and shaky for eight hours is a long time, especially if you don't see any change.

Later Mike talked about the downward spiral created when an illness characterized by feelings of hopelessness does not respond to doctors' best efforts:

I think being knocked down repeatedly, repeatedly disappointed, [is awful]. As I said to a friend of mine, "Just the impact of this illness on your life, the situations it creates, careerwise, financially, socially, relationships, your inability to see a future . . . If you put a normal person that wasn't sick in that situation, it wouldn't be very long before they were seriously depressed." . . . And if you can't get out of it because the medication doesn't work . . . I think you get to the point where the pain just far outweighs any pleasure or satisfaction. . . . When you get to the point where the illness has you in agony day after day all day long, you want to take yourself out. You're only sticking around because of the guilt trip . . . thinking . . . what impact it would have on people you love.

Like others who stumble from one drug to another, Mike became an expert on medications, often feeling that he knew more than the doctors who were treating him, particularly about his own drug regimens. I have often heard variants on Mike's observation, "When you're listening to a professional talk, they don't really get it at the depth of someone that's lived it." In my experience patients are grateful when doctors admit the incompleteness of their knowledge and the truth that their recommendation of a particular drug is largely guesswork. Mike especially admired the doctor who "when he gave me the medication . . . the first time . . . was truthful. . . . He said, 'We're playing black box medicine here. We don't really know what we're doing.'"

To illustrate how patients must sometimes take drug matters into their own hands because of doctors' lack of comprehension, Mike detailed what he had to do to discontinue Klonopin, a highly habituating medication in a family of drugs called benzodiazepines, which also includes Ativan, Xanax and Valium. He began to realize that the Klonopin, which he had been taking for anxiety, ultimately had a boomerang effect: "The first Klonopin of the day would have a good effect for about two and a half . . . hours. [However], the depression and anxiety would come back more intense, and then the next [pill] wasn't effective." He added:

> Since I had smoked and drank . . . I said [to myself], "It's bad enough to be addicted to stuff that you can go down to the corner store and get immediately if you wanted to. It's another thing to be addicted to something that you have to call up somebody [to get]." So I decided to come off the Klonopin, but I didn't tell the doctor I was going to come off it.

Mike had learned through painful experience that a drug with a very short "half-life" (the amount of time it takes for the blood level of a drug to drop by 50 percent) can shortly make you feel that you have far less than half a life.

Like Mike, I often worry about whether, after fifteen years of use, I am addicted to Klonopin. Therefore, I listened intently when Mike explained that the only way he could stop taking Klonopin was to lie to his doctor. Believing that doctors often grossly underestimate the difficulty of giving up such drugs, Mike "didn't want them deciding how fast I should be able to come off it." He tapered off the medication over several months while "I just kept getting the prescriptions. . . . I'd [even] keep track of when it was time to fill the next one and even if I had a hundred tablets left I still filled the next one." When, finally, he was no longer taking the Klonopin, he told the doctor that he wanted to stop, and, as expected, he was given a plan that would have required tapering off in three weeks. Mike expressed disbelief that doctors could be unaware of the difficulty of discontinuing an addictive drug:

> Yeah, I'm just amazed, I'm amazed. . . . Why hasn't this been figured out? Because people know about the other benzodiazepines. . . . I know someone that went through Valium withdrawal and also went through alcohol withdrawal. And he said alcohol withdrawal, which can kill you, was a piece of cake compared to getting off Valium. It took something like two and a half years and he was still reacting to it. . . . I think that the cure was worse than the illness. I think that the Klonopin . . . if it was doing something for me in the beginning, was no longer working as effectively. And it was actually making me worse with that boomerang effect. Plus, what I did notice when I got off the Klonopin is [that] my memory improved dramatically and I seemed to have less apathy, less lethargy. When I heard other people like really suffering, going through the withdrawal, and sometimes they would actually even have to go to the hospital, I was really quite pleased with myself that I had handled it that way. With all my stupidity caused by the depression and cognitive distortion and chaos, at least I thought to myself, "Well, you did yourself a favor there."

Among the few drugs in recent years that have dulled Mike's depression is an atypical antidepressant called Wellbutrin. On Wellbutrin he "felt sort of like going out and dancing and drinking and whatever else came to mind." However, as Mike found out the hard way, Wellbutrin has been known to cause mania in some people. Mike had been doing well on Wellbutrin until he reached a dose of 300 milligrams while on a trip to a neighboring state. At that point "something kicked in." He described the encroaching mania: "I felt like I was going to go through the roof. . . . [It was] almost too intense. It's almost like I wanted to escape it." Appropriately, Mike decreased the amount of Wellbutrin he was taking, but he never told his doctor what had happened when he was away. He believed that psychiatrists "are afraid of mania. They're afraid of mania and I was taking the medication that pushed me into mania or something that was very close to it. . . . So, knowing that doctors get absolutely paranoid about mania, [I said nothing]. Some doctors won't even give bipolars antidepressants. They'd rather see them go through their life depressed . . . which I think is criminal." Mike continued to experiment with dosage levels, but questions of noncompliance eventually became moot when, a few months later, the salutary effects of the Wellbutrin disappeared.

While Mike was grateful for whatever small relief he sometimes got from the "next" drug, even the best ones "still leave me in hell." He questioned the pharmaceutical companies' assertions that their drugs "work" for 80 percent of people suffering from depression. Does this include the people who experience only incremental relief, or those who trade one set of symptoms for another? The claim is misleading, Mike contended, because "people think of working as some significant and meaningful relief from pain." When I suggested that drugs sometimes only move people from the eighth to the seventh of Dante's circles of hell, Mike laughed and said, "Right. . . . You're standing on your head in the mud instead of having your toes burned. . . . It's just . . . very deceptive advertising and it's unethical."

Given his history, it is testimony to Mike's spirit and courage that he still searched for solutions. Although he continued to hope for new medications that might pierce even *his* mood disorder, at the time of our talk he was focusing on alternative treatments, particularly supplements. He used fish oil, flaxseed oil, Sami, St. John's Wort, and kava kava, among other things.

We laughed about the latest remedy he was considering—pig vitamins. Six months before our interview he had heard a grain and feed salesman talk about "a certain mix of vitamins . . . and minerals that [farmers] give to aggressive pigs. . . . Everyone's joking that . . . we're going to listen to a salesman and a pig farmer . . . and that's going to turn our life around." Apparently, though, some unorthodox doctors had taken the pig vitamins seriously, and reports on the Internet claimed astounding success. Mike was looking into the matter.

Toward the end of the interview I asked Mike the two questions I routinely asked all my interviewees: "What is the most difficult thing about using psychiatric drugs?" and "What would you most want those who read my book to know about psychiatric drug use?" Here's how Mike responded to the first question:

> I think the first thing that came to mind as the most difficult thing about taking them is the fact that they don't work [for me]. I don't think that if they worked I'd have any problems taking them. If I was feeling very well I might be even more worried about what they were going to do to my wonderful life [in terms of health] down the road. But I don't get down the road too far with them now, you know.

And about the message he wanted to convey to readers:

> I would like to have it just spelled out in plain language . . . the fact that one-third of the people respond well [to medications] and the rest don't respond well. The fact [is] that one-third don't respond at all. . . . Just get the truth out there and get it out just . . . point-blank.

Because of the difficulties in determining whether treatments "work," no one really knows the true effectiveness of either talk or drug therapies. There is no way to affirm or disprove the validity of Mike's last claim that a third of those with affective disorders are treatment resistant. What does seem clear is that responses to medications exist along a continuum from cure to failure. While we cannot know just how those who suffer from depression, anxiety, and bipolar illness are statistically arranged along this continuum, there seems little doubt that medications do not routinely cure mood disorder.

What Happens at the Hospital

Cait Irwin

Cait Irwin began her battle with depression at the age of four-teen. In her book Conquering the Beast Within, *she writes to other teens about what she has gone through and gives them encouragement for dealing with their own situations. In this excerpt she describes what it was like being hospitalized and what she learned from that experience.*

If you have to go to the hospital it will be scary at first, especially if you don't know what's going to happen. I'll tell you what happened to me. It may vary in some ways from hospital to hospital.

The reason that I needed to check into the hospital was that I got to a point when I couldn't trust myself. I didn't know if I wanted to live or die. I went to the hospital to talk about my problems and to find the right medicine to help me. But most importantly to keep me safe.

When I arrived at the hospital it was really hard to be left there. But before my mom left, we worked out a plan for phone calls. The hospital had to approve it to make sure the people I talked to were a good influence.

I was allowed two calls in the morning and two at night. I found a lot of inner courage experiencing this. My mom brought me some things from home, like my pillow and my favorite stuffed animal. The hospital staff checked everything for items which I could use to hurt myself. I got a routine check-up by the doctor who took my weight, blood pressure and all the basics.

The first night I was in there was hard. The room didn't have anything in it except a bathroom, bed and some drawers.

Cait Irwin, *Conquering the Beast Within: How I Fought Depression and Won ... and How You Can, Too.* New York: Times Books, 1998. Copyright © 1998 by Catlin Irwin. All rights reserved. Reproduced by permission.

The next morning I had to get up bright and early. The food wasn't all that hot. The staff went over the daily schedule. Then came the hard part. A total physical. That day was probably the hardest day of all because I thought I had taken every test in the book. In the hospital I received information on the various levels of progression through their program. The more my condition improved, the more freedom I received.

Here are the levels:

1. Suicide and escape precautions
2. Level two - still pretty strict
3. Level Three - more privileges
4. Level four - freedom

When you get on level four you're almost ready to go home. At first my family could only visit me for a couple of hours during the week and on weekends. The more the staff got to know me, the more I considered them as friends, rather than superiors. I had a roommate that had already been through the system so that helped.

When I was released from the hospital I became discouraged very easily because I felt vulnerable. I felt a lot of pressure to be the enthusiastic person I once was . . . the actor, the athlete.

I had to keep on going to counseling and it's hard spilling your guts to doctor after doctor, but you've got to stick with it because medicine alone won't cure you.

The counseling will help shrink your beast.

Electroconvulsive Therapy

Kitty Dukakis and Larry Tye

Kitty Dukakis is the wife of a prominent American politician. Her battle of over twenty years with depression and alcoholism has received extensive media attention. In 2001 Dukakis began electroconvulsive therapy (ECT) treatments to help her depression. This somewhat controversial therapy involves sending a burst of electricity to a patient's brain which sets off a convulsion intended to shock the brain back into balance.

In this excerpt from her book, Shock: The Healing Power of Electroconvulsive Therapy, *Dukakis discusses her immediate positive reaction to her first ECT treatment and how the treatment has helped her over a period of several years. She compares ECT to other treatments she has tried, concluding that it has been more effective than any of the other treatments. She also talks about the reactions of her husband and children as they watch how ECT has affected her.*

Next thing I know I am waking up. I am back on an upper floor of Massachusetts General Hospital, in the unit where I slept last night. I feel light-headed, groggy, the way you do when anesthesia is wearing off and you are floating in the abyss between sleep and wakefulness. I vaguely recall the anesthesiologist having had me count to ten, but I never got beyond three or four. I remember Charlie Welch and his ECT team, but am not sure I got the treatment. One clue is a slight headache, which they told me ECT might cause but which could have come from the anesthesia. Another is the goo on my hair, where they must have attached the electrodes.

There is one more sign that I did in fact have my first session of seizure therapy: I feel good—I feel alive.

Michael [Dukakis, Kitty's husband] is standing there next to the nurse as I struggle to keep my eyes open, and I give him a big grin. That surprises him right away. After a bit more dozing I am awake for good, and get dressed. Michael takes me to the car, which is in the garage attached to the hospital. I have been warned not to expect too much from any single ECT treatment, especially my first, when doctors are adjusting the dose and fine-tuning their technique to my body and mind. But I already can detect a difference. Feeling this good is truly amazing given where I am coming from, which is a very dark place that has lasted a very long time. Just last night I was so shaky I didn't trust myself to stay in my own house, so I checked in here at Mass. General. That seems like ages ago. As we head home to Brookline, I remember that it is our anniversary. Our thirty-eighth. I turn to Michael and say, "Let's go out for dinner tonight!" He asks, "What?" I say, "I'm serious. Let's do it!"

Michael and I did eat out at a restaurant that night, making an anniversary I wanted to forget into one I will remember always. I was back at the hospital on an outpatient basis the next two weeks for four more treatments. After the second one I went to the hairdresser, then a dinner party, and watched the Red Sox on TV. Over the following four years I have returned to Mass. General and Charlie seven more times.

It is not an exaggeration to say that electroconvulsive therapy has opened a new reality for me. I used to deny when a depressive episode was coming on, to myself and others. I knew how much it would hurt, how long the darkness would last. I just couldn't face it. I thought if I ignored it, it might go away on its own. Now I know there is something that will work and work quickly. It takes away the anticipation and the fear. I call Charlie as soon as I spot the gathering clouds. I also used to be unable to shake the dread even when I was feeling good, because I knew the bad feelings would return, the way they always did after eight months. ECT has wiped away that foreboding. It has given me a sense of control, of hope.

As important, ECT has gotten me off antidepressants. I withdrew slowly, with help from my doctors. Since I have been off I know the full range of my feelings. I get into the car now and put on music, the classical station. I sometimes cry because it conjures up feelings of my dad, who died on March 29, 2003. When I was a child I cried often enough and hard enough that my parents used to say, "Go get the bucket for Kitty's tears." Once I went on antidepressants I couldn't bring myself to tears, whether I was listening to music or mourning my father. The drugs somehow blocked my emotions. Once I went off I was able to read the thousand or so letters we got from people who knew and loved Dad, who had worked with him or considered themselves part of our family. I finally could grieve. I could cry. ECT let me do that. As Michael says, "You can feel your feelings again."

The side effects of antidepressants didn't stop there. They created intestinal issues for me, bowel problems. They made my mouth dry and sex more difficult. I slept more than I should have. None of those complications threatened my life, but each made it less enjoyable. All those things cleared up when I stopped taking the drugs, and it has made a huge difference to me and to my loving husband.

Speed of response is another area where ECT has made a difference. It works right away. I feel the depression beginning to lift after just one treatment, and it is gone entirely within a week to ten days. With antidepressants the effects were gradual. It took time for them to feed into my system. Sometimes it was three weeks or a month before I felt the full power of a particular medication, and even then none of the drugs worked as advertised. With ECT the effect is immediate and as powerful as promised. That's not to say I am not tired after electroconvulsive therapy. I'm not going to run the Boston

Marathon, not that I ever could. But the difference between the two treatments is dramatic.

Electroconvulsive therapy has even helped with talk therapy, strange as that may sound. I had been with Roger Weiss, my therapist for five or six years. After ECT, I was able to work on issues that I couldn't before, with him and on my own. I stopped smoking fifteen months ago and feel terrific about that. I am working on my road rage, which is especially challenging every winter when we head to L.A. and start driving those confounding freeways. I am trying to stop or at least streamline my impulsive shopping and to curb my compulsion for candy and other sweets. I am even addressing what my kids call my sense of entitlement. They kid me for behaving like the "queen bee." It is not ECT per se that is curing me of those bad habits. It is staying well enough for long enough that I can start looking at behaviors I want to change. Why, for instance, do I always introduce myself by my last name as well as first? Kara, Andrea, and John say I am seeking the recognition that comes with the name Dukakis. Whether they are right or not, it was impossible to acknowledge they might be when I was depressed. I wasn't thinking clearly. ECT unfogs your head enough to face issues more honestly.

It isn't just me who sees these differences. Corky, my support group sponsor, calls the effect it has had on me "fabulous," adding that "without ECT I think you eventually might have done away with your life, maybe not on purpose, but through drinking or something. I don't think you would have had four years of sobriety without ECT." After my treatments my dad used to tell Michael, "The other Kitty is back. The good Kitty." Wilma Greenfield, a friend since we were both thirteen, says she, too, despaired that when I was depressed everything about me seemed dulled down. "The new image— the post-ECT one," she says, "is the Kitty I knew when we were growing up together. You return to that very upbeat, very positive person. The sparkle is there. There are no dips."

The kids are more skeptical, having seen me go up, then dip down, with earlier treatments. But John still concludes that ECT has "made a huge difference." Kara says, "I definitely buy into the idea that it's working, at least for now." Andrea worries every time I get ECT that that might be the time when it won't work, but so far those fears have not been borne out.

Michael is less reticent. He knows how self-destructive I was, and how nothing else seemed to help. ECT, he says, is our miracle.

That does not mean I look forward to the treatments. Who would? No one wants electricity, shot into their brain, or even to get anesthesia. But when I lie down I know that within seconds I'll be asleep—and that this process is going to make me better. I also know that, like many patients today, I can go home after each treatment rather than stay overnight in the hospital, which makes an enormous difference. That first treatment on our wedding anniversary set the pattern. It lifted the shade on my dark mood. I can be a basket case, but the first ECT always brings me out of that. The next one helps a little more, and the several after that. By the time I was finished with that first series of five, I was myself again.

I have had seven more sets of ECT at Mass. General since the first in 2001, and one at Cedars-Sinai Medical Center in Los Angeles. Some things are the same each time. I stop eating or drinking at midnight the night before, same as I would for any surgery. I am always the first patient in the morning, at seven o'clock, which Dr. Welch arranges to protect my privacy. I always start out at Phillips House, a VIP area in the hospital where I am unlikely to run into other patients and nothing gets put in my regular hospital record. I change out of street clothes into hospital pajamas, then head down in the elevator with Dr. Welch or his associate to the treatment room. I always end up back in that private room in Phillips House where I can fully wake up. I am grateful. Friends who have had ECT tell me they hated waking up in a cubicle with eight or ten patients in different cubicles around them. Hearing noises, they say, is very frightening. Your memory is shaky at that stage, and the last thing you want is anything unfamiliar, anything that might be scary.

One last thing about my experience with ECT: I am never nervous. The minute I lie down on that table the anxiety is just not there, period. It's not part of my thinking. I know I am going to start feeling better almost right away. I actually wake up hungry, and after a short nap in the hospital I can't wait to get home and have breakfast. Knowing all that helps me get prepared. I have absolute confidence in the team at Mass. General and in the procedure.

Before they begin, Charlie and his colleagues take a series of medical precautions, some of which are particular to me. I get beta-blockers to ensure there is no spike in my blood pressure or cardiac rate. They have raised my dosage of anesthesia because in the early treatments I was waking up a bit early. I get a dose of analgesic to prevent me from getting stiff, which is a special risk since I had serious neck surgery nearly twenty years ago. They wait until I am falling asleep to apply the oxygen mask, because when they did it while I was awake, it dredged up scary memories of the tonsillectomy I had in my own home as a young child. For a while I was getting a tranquilizer because I had some problems with anxiety.

All my treatments have been unilateral, which means the electrodes go on just one side of my head in positions that Charlie says are aimed at minimizing memory loss. The same concern led them to gradually lower the intensity of the stimulus they give me, to a level the doctors say is one-tenth of what Stelian Dukakis [brother of Michael Dukakis] probably got in the 1950s. Charlie also has adjusted the waveform of the current to one he says is less vigorous but still strong enough to work for me.

I generally need treatment every seven or eight months, which has always been my timeline for depression returning. It was a full fourteen months between my first and second sets of ECT, which felt great. Several times I have needed another round after just two or three months. Charlie says that is because he and I were experimenting to see whether we could get away with fewer than the normal seven treatments per series, or at least space them farther apart. He also was testing just how low-intensity he could go to minimize the chance of side effects while preserving the ECT's effectiveness. My last set was in April–May of 2005, seven and a half months after the previous one, and I have been doing great since then.

One strange effect that ECT has had on me is to leave me a little hyper. My sister notices how quickly I go back to shopping and spending money on clothing and other things. I can hear Jinny say, "Are you sure you need that?" The answer, of course, is "No, but I want it," a response that alarms my parsimonious spouse. I'm somewhat embarrassed by my free-spending ways and am working on staying away from stores, at least in the aftermath of my treatments. Roger, my therapist, says ECT can actually induce a mild mania, and that it appears to do that with me the same way antidepressants did. Maybe it is just revealing my bipolar personality, with mania naturally following the depression. Whatever it is, the mania is better than the despair and doesn't last long or create real problems. Andrea notices that I call her and my other kids at least once a day after ECT brings me out of depression—and she says they have a hard time getting me off the phone. I want to know everything they are doing, and all about my six grandkids. Speaking of the grandkids, I love being with them more than anything, but can't really be when I am deep in a depression. ECT lets me get back to myself quicker than before, and get back with my grandchildren.

A nun who contacted me after a story on my ECT appeared in the *Boston Globe* described how afraid she had been to have ECT. She said, "This is the way I would feel going in for a root canal." As for me, I hate fillings, and don't like to go to the dentist, period. I happened to have had a root canal not long before my first electroconvulsive therapy. In some ways ECT is less traumatic for me than going to the dentist, and certainly less frightening than the root canal. Lots of doctors say I am crazy for thinking something like that, but I don't have negative thoughts about the treatment.

SOCIAL ISSUES
FIRSTHAND

CHAPTER 4

How Depression
Affects Others

Living with a Monster

Kenneth Richard Fox

Kenneth and Wendy Fox were a happily married couple. Sometime after the birth of their second child, Wendy began displaying symptoms of depression, which later turned into manic depression. She started seeing psychiatrists, but whenever one recommended serious treatment, Wendy would stop seeing that doctor and seek out another, in denial of her problems. Over time she became angry and abusive, physically attacking her husband twenty-five times over a period of two years.

In the following article Kenneth Richard Fox describes what it was like living with an angry, manic-depressive wife. He points out how he was unable to force her to get treatment. Each time he reported her physical abuse to the police, they would offer to arrest her. And each time he refused because saw her not as a criminal, but as someone with an illness needing medical attention. He talks about the role that Wendy's many psychiatrists played in the continuation of her illness, and he takes responsibility for his own role in the perpetuation of her illness and her denial.

I was driving about 35 miles per hour when, out of the corner of my right eye, I saw a shiny reflection coming directly toward my chest. I grabbed for the forearm and stopped the blade just inches away. My other hand grasped the steering wheel, barely keeping the car from going into a ravine, while my right foot hit the brake.

Wendy and I had met ten years earlier, near the end of my medical residency, and there were times that I thought it had been a match made in heaven. David, our second child, had just arrived when the first signs of Wendy's illness appeared.

Our eldest, Kim, was just over three, and the four of us seemed to be the perfect family. Kim was fantastic, and I expected little less from David. I was an eye surgeon and Wendy a speech pathologist. We were, I thought, well established in the community with a nice circle of friends.

Wendy had always been full of energy, positive and forward-looking, highly social, very solid and responsible. People came to know her for these qualities, and I felt very lucky to have her as my wife and best friend.

First Signs of Depression

In the early days after David's birth, Wendy was understandably not quite the same as before; she had two handfuls of responsibility. She began to cancel some professional appointments. Wendy had also been very active in a number of organizations, and, in time, some of that slowed, too.

I was working long hours, so it wasn't until David's first birthday that I realized my wife had developed a habit of sleeping in and leaving his morning care to our live-in nanny. Wendy, who used to insist on doing everything herself, was doing a lot less. She was tired and short-tempered but insisted nothing was wrong. She had a physical examination, and her doctor said she was in good shape.

A couple of years passed. Wendy was still tired and irritable, and she often couldn't sleep through the night. She started seeing psychiatrists. She was diagnosed with severe depression, which may have been triggered by our son's birth. Most of her doctors were reluctant to tell me any more than that because I was the spouse, not the patient, even though I was a professional colleague. Something significant was intruding into our lives, separating us and dividing the family, and her doctors were throwing a cloak of professional silence over it.

The Darkness of Depression

Wendy went through about ten psychiatrists that I knew about. She stopped filing insurance claims, so I had no way to know who she was seeing or any further diagnosis. She was secretive about what her medication was and whether she was taking it. If she was on medication, I couldn't tell the difference. She fluctuated between denying that anything was wrong and being overwhelmed by shame about her problem. When a psychiatrist proposed electroshock therapy or hospitalization, she'd stop seeing him only to find another, searching for one who would tell her that she was okay.

Her father, it turned out, had suffered from major depression, caused by a chemical imbalance in the brain, before he descended into manic depression. This disease, also known as bipolar disorder, tosses the sufferer between extreme highs and lows. Wendy's father died when she was a teenager. She had told me he died of a heart attack, but I later found out he had committed suicide and her family had moved away in part because they felt disgraced.

He used to beat her and perhaps her older sister, Sharon, who also suffered from major depression. Wendy would never admit any of this; from what I was able to understand, she never discussed these issues with her psychiatrists.

Her greatest fear was of becoming "like her father." Her other fear was that she would lose her children. The time came when she sometimes no longer knew what was real. As her depression deepened into manic depression, my wife had become just like her father.

A few of the doctors who didn't mind discussing the problem with me said they had urged Wendy to tell the children, and that she and no one else had to tell them. The point of this had not only to do with her parenting but also her inheritance of this disease. But she never did. She was afraid that if they or anyone else knew, she might lose her family and then even kill herself.

Wendy tried to commit suicide at least once by taking an overdose of pills. I came home from work late one night and found her befuddled and nearly unconscious. I believe if I had not been there, she might not have made it through the night.

Though I was a doctor, there was pitifully little I could do to help my wife, our children, and myself. All of us were suffering.

When she descended into manic depression, Wendy became at times paranoid and delusional and didn't trust anyone. She projected things she thought or did onto other people. As the person closest to her, I became her prime target.

Anger Against Herself and Others

She was a monolith of anger. In the major depression years, she turned her anger against herself. In the bipolar years, she heaped her anger on others, mostly on those nearest to her.

She accused me and other people of trying to alienate our children from her, steal her money, damage her speech therapy practice, destroy her friendships, drive her crazy, hurt her, and ruin her reputation. Everyone was out to get her.

By the time David was four, Wendy was much less able to work or care for the children. I sold my medical practice shortly thereafter to devote more of my time to this crisis and to taking care of my family. I didn't know what else to do.

Husband Gets Help for Himself

I joined a support group for spouses and other family members of manic-depressives and started seeing a therapist, one whom Wendy and I had gone to early on and she had discarded. I wasn't alone anymore; there were others who understood the depth of my despair in this situation. I began to appreciate and understand that others suffer with this same problem all too often.

I began the long, slow process of emerging from "codependence," living the same anguished existence as the partner-patient, like being stuck in the same box with her. The code-pendent partner needs to break out to stay healthy. I sought to regain my own self-confidence. It was a slow and difficult process. In time, I started to see things more clearly.

After six years of illness, my wife suddenly went into re-mission. We were able to love again, and life seemed wonderful once more. I began then to think that the manic depression had cured itself.

A year later, the seesaw tipped the other way. The relapse into full-blown bipolar disorder came hard and fast. In the manic phase, Wendy felt better, the black hole of despair went away. There was no stopping her. She was on the move. She got things done. But she was a raving lunatic, which became increasingly apparent to just about everyone she knew. Most of our friends became somewhat more distant. The relatively few friendships that withstood the test of that long period were sweet, indeed, and helped me a lot.

The family therapist we went to at that time threw up his hands, unable to deal with Wendy's anger and abuse. She also had run-ins with authority figures. Wendy crushed anything that got in the way of her systematic denial.

To treat the mania is to risk the return of the depression, a kind of overcorrection. No one in his "wrong mind" would want to do that. Behavior during mania is laced with uncon-trollable and dangerous excesses that may include violence, hypersexual activity, insomnia, overworking, overspending, or other extreme behaviors. Manic-depressives often seem normal to people they meet casually. For those who see more of them, the problem is usually unmistakable.

Violent Anger

However bad or daunting the major depression had been for me and the children, this mania seemed a hundred times worse. Wendy vented her anger through violence, most often against me but sometimes against our son and other people.

In her delusions she believed that almost everyone around her was evil or potentially harmful to her.

After shedding so many psychiatrists along the way, she eventually found a quack psychotherapist who seemed perfectly satisfied to see her for about ten minutes once a month and ask if she was okay. Of course, to herself, she was just fine. This pseudosupport kept her going for a while. He was a far cry from the psychiatrists who wanted to hospitalize her and start major drug or even electroshock therapy. She felt encouraged. The trouble was, this "treatment" was encouraging the monster that was destroying the wife I loved. It is the oddest feeling when this kind of mental illness, this intangible and overpowering force, comes between you and someone you love dearly.

I spent about eleven years in all trying to deal with one phase of her illness or another and seeing our children suffer because of it. When they grew older, she would sometimes tell Kim or even David that she was just "a little down."

Wendy was a prisoner of her brain chemistry. Our kids lived in a house of horrors for much of their formative years and may also have inherited the propensity for the disease from their mother. I was married to the monster that had taken over my wife and my children's mother.

In the last two years of our hellish relationship, my wife physically assaulted me no fewer than twenty-five times. I wound up bruised, scalded, and cut just about every few weeks. These unprovoked attacks even sometimes occurred when I was sleeping. I reported each episode to the police, who wanted to arrest my wife. I refused. I didn't see the criminal justice system as a solution; I didn't see my wife as a criminal but as someone who was very sick. A female police officer who responded to one of my calls told me that her male policeman partner had also been the victim of a petite but physically abusive wife with apparently a very similar illness who wound up in jail.

The twenty-sixth and final violent episode was an apparently premeditated attempt on my life, with a kitchen knife, while I was driving. That was the blow that ultimately ended our marriage. I had to save myself, but I couldn't help her or the children.

Public Help Is Ineffective

I blame my medical colleagues and those in the other helping professions in part for not being aggressive enough about diagnosing, investigating, and treating this type of mental illness, especially in potentially dangerous cases such as this one was. True, doctors are bound by the patient privilege doctrine, but they are at the same time sometimes the only ones privy to the potential public safety menace that certain of these more violent patients represent. Just as psychiatrists should act to attempt to prevent a suicide, there must be a mechanism for them to suggest to some authority the violent tendencies of certain patients they may see. Only in this manner can these patients be protected from their own destruction or from harming others. In Wendy's case, her extreme denial and the fact that she frequently would change psychiatrists were severe confounding factors in both providing her with more and better treatment and in protecting those around her. However, the level of awareness of psychiatrists in contact professionally with these types of patients must remain very high so that they may see through that cloudy veil worn by patients in denial.

The public "safety net"—police, courts, and social welfare agencies—is also often most unhelpful. Although my own initial reticence to bring my wife into the criminal justice system in the face of her repeated violent episodes was probably not helpful in the long run, once it became quite apparent that there was something drastically wrong, things did not get any better. The U.S. Attorney's office charged with prosecuting Wendy was ultimately cajoled into dismissing the serious assault charge against her because the specter of trying her and in the process interjecting our two children even more into the middle of what was a very ugly situation was highly unappealing.

Taking a singleminded and thoroughly unenlightened view of all of this, the divorce court simply ignored Wendy's significant mental health history, unwilling to require an independent medical evaluation that might have led to an attempt to moderate or modify her violent behavior. That might well have ultimately led to her hospitalization for a trial of medicines or other therapy such as electric shock treatment. That court also was unable to bring itself to separate the potentially dangerous mother from her minor children until sufficient medical remediation of the condition had been accomplished. By allowing the severe adverse effects of a pathologically angry and violent mother to persist in the home, her two minor children left in contact with her, the children were doomed to suffer long-standing adverse psychological effects. The system makes it virtually impossible to privately bring an action to involuntarily commit these types of individuals. Generally, several psychiatrists have to testify that they have personally seen solid evidence of the worst of the violent behavior; given the denial, the lack of compliance, and proper follow-up in this instance and in others like it this standard is most unlikely to often be met.

I feel strongly that we must do much more for people with severe depression and/or bipolar disorder. When they are thoroughly uncontrolled, we must do something to them to protect both themselves and the rest of us in their midst. Year by year we learn more about this common but sometimes violent disorder and the havoc that it visits upon individuals, families, and society. Doctors involved in treating these patients need to be as proactive as possible. Judges ought to be further educated about the horrible potential consequences of this condition; the law must generously and require them to act in the best interests of minor children but also protect those patients and loved ones around them from the ravages of this disease. The police need to understand more about bipolar disorder and its many faces; social service networks that interface with these people also should act in a more inspired and proactive fashion in their dealings with them.

Caring for a Depressed Husband

Cheri Fuller

Cheri Fuller's husband, Holmes, suffered from depression for many years before finally being diagnosed and treated. The treatment itself took several years before he was able to function normally again. Speaking from a Christian perspective and relying on her own experience and the experience of other women like her, Fuller lists some pointers for women whose husbands are suffering from depression. She describes ways to be supportive and encouraging as a husband proceeds in recovery. She also makes suggestions to women about how to care for themselves and their children while caring for their husbands.

Several years ago, my husband, Holmes, began skipping meals and losing weight, eventually 25 pounds within three months. His laid-back, somewhat pensive temperament turned irritable and moody. Although he typically was quiet about his feelings, Holmes became increasingly withdrawn and didn't seem to enjoy things anymore.

I knew Holmes was encountering tough times as a home-builder in a flagging economy and a tanking stock market. But I kept hoping he'd perk up if he got another construction job. In the meantime, being ever the encourager, I tried everything I could think of to cheer him up. I pointed out all the positive things he did, such as being a great dad or helping other people. I encouraged Holmes to look ahead to a family trip we'd planned, but that didn't help, either. As the months rolled into years, neither my encouraging words nor my hard work to take up the slack in our income seemed to make a difference.

Cheri Fuller, "When Your Husband Struggles with Depression: Take Heart—There's Hope for Him and You," *Today's Christian Woman*, September–October 2003, pp. 68–72. Reproduced by permission of the author, www.cherifuller.com.

In 1995, roughly seven years after I first noticed my husband's struggles, our pastor realized from a conversation with Holmes that he was suicidal. He immediately made Holmes an appointment with a doctor who diagnosed him as having clinical depression. The physician told us Holmes probably had been depressed for years. Situational depression caused by the crushing pressures of Holmes's declining building business in the late 1980s, compounded by a genetic predisposition to clinical depression on both sides of his family, had pushed him to the edge. Perhaps if I'd known the clues, Holmes could have gotten help before his depression had become full-blown.

I've discovered I'm not the only woman who's experienced life with a depressed husband. With an unstable economy and corporate meltdowns, depression in males is on the rise. That means countless wives face the challenge of trying to help a spouse who's in emotional turmoil. But depression doesn't have to bring down your entire family. There is help, there is hope, and there are ways you can support your spouse—and yourself.

Caring for Your Husband

If the dark cloud of depression overtakes your spouse, how can you help him?

Recognize the signs. It's important to distinguish between *situational* depression triggered by something such as a job layoff or demotion, and *clinical* depression. Situational depression involves some of the same symptoms of clinical depression ... but they're of shorter duration and lower intensity. For example, if your husband's depression is caused by discouragement over a job loss, within six months he should regroup, recover his enjoyment of life, and move on. However, according to Michael Navarro, a licensed psychotherapist, clinical depression's symptoms are more pronounced and last far longer. The absence of pleasure in the activities your husband once enjoyed is greater; his malaise, anger, or weight loss more substantial.

If your husband experiences a majority of the symptoms of depression, he needs professional help. Your family physician can determine what's biological and what's psychological; he may make a diagnosis of clinical depression and refer your spouse to a psychologist or psychiatrist for therapy and medication. In Holmes's case, counseling and an antidepressant were helpful short-term, but since we didn't have the money to continue therapy, his recovery process took much longer. (I've since learned many good therapists provide a sliding fee scale depending on your financial condition.)

How would you know if your husband needs to be hospitalized? If he's seeing a doctor, his physician would make that recommendation. But here are other clues that in-patient help is needed to stabilize your spouse: when he repeatedly cancels or doesn't show up for his outpatient/counseling appointments or refuses help; when he digresses into a more nonfunctional state; or if he experiences severe weight loss or sudden gain. And—most important—if he makes statements such as, "I wish I wasn't around," or "I think it's better if you collect my insurance. You and the kids would be better off without me," which indicate suicidal thinking.

Accept and love your spouse. One of the most important things you can do for your struggling mate is to let him know you still love and accept him despite how he feels about himself. "I'm not saying accepting is easy," says psychologist Archibald Hart, author of *Dark Clouds, Silver Linings.* "But you have to accept the reality of the problem. It's there whether you like it or not, and your responsibility is to communicate love and acceptance in whatever way you possibly can." This could include a loving touch or hug, or gentle encouragement through a card or meaningful gift.

During one of Holmes's darkest days, he said, "We—and I—may never be happy again; you'd be better off leaving." I went in the other room, wept, and prayed for strength and the right response. A short time later, I sat down by Holmes, held his hand, and said, "Even if we're never happy again, it's just not all about happiness; it's about loving each other and being together. I'm committed to you for the rest of our lives. I'm not going anywhere." Although we had huge hills yet to climb, that was a turning point for us. And in that particular response, Holmes felt unconditionally loved and accepted right where he was.

Encourage exercise. While physical exercise can be an extra challenge to those struggling with depression, the endorphins it provides create a natural mood-lifter. So gently encourage your husband to go for a walk with you after dinner as many nights as he's willing, or to work out at a gym or do whatever activity he enjoys most when he feels up to it. When my husband and I took our evening walks, he sometimes would open up. One night as we walked, I asked Holmes to give me a word picture of how he felt.

"I feel like a vine's wrapping itself around me; that it began at my feet and now is almost up to my neck, choking me," he described. It was hard to hear how terrible he felt, but it helped me connect with him and understand a little of what he was going through.

Realize anger often accompanies depression. But don't allow your husband to disrespect or abuse you or your children. Be available to listen, but avoid trying to be his therapist. "A mate's role is primarily one of support. The main therapeutic work needs to be done by a professional," says Hart.

Whether your husband's anger is rooted in grief and loss issues, unresolved childhood issues, failure, or job loss, he needs someone with whom to talk. One counselor I know has her clients list ten things they're angry about when they come in for therapy because she's found that underneath most depression is anger over something.

Encourage fellowship with other men. When Carrie's husband, Jeremy, went through a depressive period after a job loss, a small group of friends met with him weekly over coffee to be his sounding board for his job-hunting. They also kept him in their prayers during the difficult months. Their support was invaluable to his recovery and the new career direction he found.

Avoid using words that make him feel worse. A man in the doldrums of depression doesn't need to hear, "How can you be depressed with all God has done in our lives?" (He's probably already feeling as though no one understands, and this just confirms it.) Avoid preaching: "Just read your Bible more and get right with God, and your depression will go away."

Refrain from belittling him or comparing him to others as in, "You know, Brian took St. John's Wort and he bounced back from his depression in only three months." Also avoid saying, "Look on the bright side. Count yourself lucky and cheer up," which makes him feel guilty. One woman I know purposed to praise her husband for the baby steps he took in learning to trust God in the darkness, and didn't blurt out, "I thought you already knew that!" when he shared insights with her.

Caring for Yourself

I became so emotionally and physically depleted during my husband's depression that I began suffering from severe insomnia. While working overtime, I parented our teens and worried about our financial situation and my husband. Sometimes I felt abandoned by Holmes—emotionally, at least. Eventually I realized I harbored some anger as well. Some sessions with a counselor and later a small support group helped me tremendously.

If you get support and deal with your issues, you'll be healthier emotionally and thus better able to help your husband and children. Here are some ways:

Ask for help. When Brenda's husband, Daryle, needed to be hospitalized for severe depression, she didn't think to ask her brother or pastor to accompany her. She drove Daryle the three hours to the center by herself.

Mile after mile he protested, "I'm going home. I'm not going to the hospital. The bank will pull the loans if I'm gone. The company will go under. We'll lose everything." After Brenda got her husband in the hospital and almost collapsed from exhaustion, she realized she couldn't do everything alone. She found a student teacher to live with her family temporarily to help with her children and take them to school. Brenda learned to ask others for help. In the same way, you may need help from a support group or prayer partners, and assistance with your children.

Consider counseling with your husband's therapist, because frequently the wife feels responsible for her husband's depression. Find one trusted friend with whom you can cry, be real, and pray. Flo Perkins, an elderly friend whose husband had suffered with chronic depression, was my lifesaver. Flo understood, listened, prayed for me, and encouraged me repeatedly. She passed on the comfort with which God had comforted her (2 Corinthians 1:3–4). From her I learned the invaluable truth that I could give the Lord all my troubles and entrust my husband to his care.

Don't keep secrets. When Liz's husband's life crashed around him due to clinical depression, they went from being pillars in their rural community to being under the lowest rock. He lost his profession, his reputation, his earning power, and his hope as he lived for six long years in a state of depression. One of the best things they did was endeavor to keep open communication with each other and their kids. They held family councils and talked over what was happening in age-appropriate ways, praying together during crises and ongoing struggles.

A word of caution: It's best to clear this kind of family meeting first with your husband, perhaps by saying, "You've always been such a loving dad. Could you help me talk to the kids about your depression to let them know it's not their fault, and that we're all going to be healing together?" Avoid saying, "Your depression's hurting our children, messing their lives up, and making life hard," which only will make him feel worse. If he prefers, you could sit down with your children alone and explain the nature of depression and that you'll help them cope with their dad's condition.

Your kids may need to talk to someone such as a youth pastor or counselor who can help them sort through their feelings. They also need to know they always can come to you to talk about the situation.

Remind yourself of God's truth. When Brenda was beset by fears, time after time she told herself the truths that restored her stability: that God would never leave or forsake her (Hebrews 13:5); that he promised her his grace when she was weak (2 Corinthians 12:10); and that God somehow would weave everything—even this depression—into a pattern for good (Romans 8:28).

"So often we try to force our way out of a crisis," Brenda says. "Instead, I began to embrace the situation and say, 'Okay, God, what do you want me to learn in this? How do you want me to change? And what are you going to accomplish in my husband and family through this difficult time?'"

As she focused on God, Brenda saw him working through Daryle's hospitalization, the friends who surrounded Daryle, and the spiritual growth they as a couple experienced. Before, Daryle had been Brenda's rock; through this experience, Brenda learned to depend more on God. And as Daryle recovered, he developed an effective ministry with hurting people and a special sensitivity to those suffering from depression.

Take "mini-vacations." During the six years her husband was depressed, Liz learned to create brief getaways from her family difficulties. Since they were financially challenged, Liz took long walks through the countryside, singing hymns and praise choruses, sometimes crying buckets of tears and other times stopping to journal her feelings. She lit scented candles at home and took bubble baths to relax. She planned fun activities for her children—picnics, outings to the state park, zoo, and movies, and occasional trips to the grandparents—and carried them out without her husband's participation when he couldn't even fake the energy to be involved. These short breaks refueled Liz for the challenges she faced.

Let prayer be your lifeline. "Praying for those we love who are depressed is our best hope," says Gerry Mensch, who not only survived her own depression but her husband's as well. "Antidepressants can help, but some in the grip of depression refuse to seek help. When God begins to work in their hearts, he'll accomplish more than we or medication ever can." If your husband won't go for counseling, start praying he'll wake up and ask for assistance, or that God will put a man in his life to steer him toward help.

Throughout Holmes's depression, my lifeline was praying Scriptures for him such as Joel 2:25, which asks God to restore the wasted years; Colossians 1:9–12, to give my husband direction; Isaiah 61:1–3, to lift his heaviness of despair and replace it with praise and joy; and 1 Peter 4:8, to fill *me* with the love that covers a multitude of sins.

It took several years for Holmes to recover from depression, and as we prayed together, we experienced God's grace for every situation we faced. Prayer strengthened our marriage when we were weak, and reminded us again and again of God's love. While Holmes's recovery wasn't quick, God always was faithful. Although medication and counseling helped, God's healing power and his Word kept us together.

Today, when I see Holmes smile as he holds one of our five grandchildren, sense his sheer enjoyment of an American history course he recently took at a local university, or experience the fun of strolling on the beach together, I'm grateful for where he is now. I'm thankful for the things we learned and the comfort we received from God and others. I'm also glad we have a chance to share what we learned with others going through depression.

Confronting a Coworker About His Illness

"Dr. Ursus"

"Dr. Ursus" is a pseudonym of a Canadian medical doctor. In this article, he talks about noticing symptoms of depression gradually appearing in a fellow doctor, Dr. Lente. When a nurse mentioned that she and other nurses had noticed symptoms, he realized it was his responsibility as a doctor and as a friend to report Dr. Lente's behavior and to help him get treatment. He spoke with Dr. Lente, who quietly assented to his need for help.

It started a few months ago. I noticed Dr. Lente's rack of unfinished charts piling up, heard whispers about unchecked lab results, saw his gait begin to slow and trundle, watched him avoid eye contact with colleagues and patients. Even his voice seemed to go down in volume, so that one had to strain to hear him. He was gradually withdrawing from everyone.

He never took any sick time—I would know, since I'd have to cover some of his shifts—and he completed his share of emergency shifts and call days. He was still doing the work he was supposed to be doing. As to whether he was doing it properly, I didn't know, although his averted eyes and barely audible voice suggested a serious problem.

A senior nurse came to me, pointing out the symptoms I had noticed myself. She said she was merely a representative, that many of the nurses felt the same way, and that patients were mentioning that Dr. Lente seemed "very strange," "different" and "odd."

My impulse was to say, "Talk to the department head, it's his job to deal with this kind of thing." But that wouldn't have been a satisfactory response from a friend. After all, I did care about Norman. I wanted him to be the good doctor he once was, not the uncommunicative, lost soul he seemed to be now. I also feared for what would happen if his behaviour got the attention of the department head. Would his privileges be revoked? Would he have an income? Would he be reported to the College? I looked at the nurse and said, "I'll talk to him."

That night I did a MEDLINE search on "depression" and "physicians." I also looked up the physician professional support Web site. And what I learned confirmed what I already knew but wanted to avoid: that I had a duty to report impaired behaviour in any of my colleagues for their own good and for the good of the public. By contacting the physician support people I was immediately putting the sick physician in contact with all the resources—family doctors, psychiatrists, counsellors, Caduceus groups, urine monitoring—they would need to get well. There was also one other message: that it was lonely to be a suffering ill person.

I was going to have to turn him in.

The next day I caught him as he entered the staff lounge. I insisted on buying him a coffee at the cafeteria. As we walked there, I noticed his loping gait, his unwillingness to make eye contact, his rather messy state of dress. When we sat down, I asked him as gently as I could, "Norman, what's wrong?"

I was unsure of myself. Who was I to ask personal questions? I expected denial. I expected anger. I expected him to say there was nothing wrong, that I should leave him alone. But, in the end, I didn't have to drag in the observations of the nurses or indirect patient complaints; all I had to do was listen, though I had to strain to hear the long, slow words.

"I'm feeling tired all the time. I can't concentrate to the point that I'm anxious I'll make a mistake at work. I don't know what to do about it; it just gets worse every day. Now it's so bad I don't want to wake up."

I told Norman that he should see our local psychiatrist and that I would arrange a rapid referral. And I told him the part that was the most difficult to say: that I would report his obvious mental difficulty to the professional support program.

To my surprise, there were no denunciations. Just a slight, almost imperceptible nod, as if he must have known what was coming.

Organizations to Contact

The editors have compiled the following list of organizations concerned with the issues debated in this book. The descriptions are derived from materials provided by the organizations. All have publications or information available for interested readers. The list was compiled on the date of publication of the present volume; the information provided here may change. Be aware that many organizations take several weeks or longer to respond to inquiries, so allow as much time as possible.

American Academy of Child and
Adolescent Psychiatry (AACAP)
3615 Wisconsin Avenue NW, Washington, DC   20016-3007
(202) 966-7300 • Fax: (202) 966-2891
e-mail: communications@aacap.org
Web site: www.aacap.org

The American Academy of Child and Adolescent Psychiatry (AACAP) is a national, professional medical association dedicated to treating and improving the quality of life for children, adolescents, and families affected by psychiatric disorders. The AACAP distributes information in an effort to promote an understanding of mental illnesses and remove the stigma associated with them, advance efforts in prevention of mental illnesses, and assure proper treatment and access to services for children and adolescents.

American Association of Suicidology (AAS)
5221 Wisconsin Avenue NW, Washington, DC   20015
(202) 237-2280 • Fax: (202) 237-2282
e-mail: info@suicidology.org
Web site: www.suicidology.org

The goal of the American Association of Suicidology (AAS) is to understand and prevent suicide. AAS promotes research, public awareness programs, public education, and training for professionals and volunteers. In addition, AAS serves as a national clearinghouse for information on suicide. The membership of AAS includes mental health and public health professionals, researchers, suicide prevention and crisis intervention centers, school districts, crisis center volunteers, survivors of suicide, and a variety of laypersons interested in suicide prevention.

American Psychiatric Association (APA)
1000 Wilson Boulevard, Suite 1825
Arlington, VA   22209-3901
(703) 907-7300
e-mail: apa@psych.org
Web site: www.psych.org

The American Psychiatric Association is an organization of psychiatrists working together to ensure humane care and effective treatment for all persons with mental disorders, including mental retardation and substance-related disorders.

American Psychological Association (APA)
750 First Street NE, Washington, DC   20002-4242
(800) 374-2721
e-mail: public.affairs@apa.org
Web site: www.apa.org

The American Psychological Association is a scientific and professional organization. Its purpose is to advance psychology as a science and profession and as a means of promoting health, education, and human welfare.

Bipolar Disorders Clinic, Stanford University School of Medicine
401 Quarry Road, Stanford, CA   94305-5723
(650) 724-4795 • Fax: (650) 723-2507
e-mail: bipolar@med.stanford.edu
Web site: http://bipolar.stanford.edu

The Bipolar Disorders Clinic is part of the Department of Psychiatry and Behavioral Sciences at Stanford University School of Medicine. The clinic offers ongoing clinical treatment, manages clinical trials, presents lectures and seminar courses at Stanford University, and trains residents in the School of Medicine. Its Web site provides useful information on bipolar disorder.

Child and Adolescent Bipolar Foundation (CABF)
1000 Skokie, Suite 570, Wilmette, IL   60091
(847) 256-8525 • Fax: (847) 920-9498
e-mail: cabf@bpkids.org
Web site: www.bpkids.org

The Child and Adolescent Bipolar Foundation is a parent-led, not-for-profit, Web-based membership organization of families raising children diagnosed with, or at risk for, pediatric bipolar disorder.

Depression and Bipolar Support Alliance (DBSA)
730 Franklin Street, Suite 501, Chicago, IL   60610-7224
(800) 826-3632 • Fax: (312) 642-7243
e-mail: info@dbsalliance.org
Web site: www.dbsalliance.org

The Depression and Bipolar Support Alliance (DBSA) is a nonprofit, patient-directed organization focusing on depression and bipolar disorder. The organization fosters an understanding of these life-threatening illnesses by providing up-to-date, scientifically based educational materials written in language the general public can understand. Through political advocacy activities, the organization works to ensure that people living with mood disorders are treated equitably. DBSA has over one thousand patient-run support groups across the United States.

Families for Depression Awareness
395 Totten Pond Road, Suite 404, Waltham, MA   02451
(781) 890-0220 • Fax: (781) 890-2411
e-mail: info@familyaware.org
Web site: www.familyaware.org

Families for Depression Awareness is a nonprofit organization that helps families, especially family caregivers and friends, recognize and cope with unipolar and bipolar depression. The organization provides educational materials, outreach, and advocacy to support families and friends. Families for Depression Awareness is made up of families who have lost a family member to suicide or have watched a loved one suffer with depression.

International Foundation for Research and Education on Depression (iFred)
2017-D Renard Court, Annapolis, MD   21401
(410) 268-0044 • Fax: (443) 782-0739
e-mail: info@ifred.org
Web site: www.ifred.org

The International Foundation for Research and Education on Depression (iFred), is a nonprofit organization dedicated to researching causes of depression, supporting those dealing with depression, and combating the stigma associated with depression. iFred's primary goal is to bring energy and information together from a variety of existing sources to educate, inform, and change public perceptions of depression.

National Alliance on Mental Illness (NAMI)
2107 Wilson, Suite 300, Arlington, VA   22201-3042
(703) 524-7600 • Fax: (703) 524-9094
e-mail: info@nami.org
Web site: www.nami.org

The National Alliance on Mental Illness (NAMI) is a grassroots mental health organization dedicated to improving the lives of persons living with serious mental illness and their families. NAMI organizations in every state and in local communities across the country join together to meet the NAMI mission through advocacy, research, support, and education. NAMI provides a toll-free telephone help line, conducts public awareness activities, and sponsors a speakers' bureau on mental illness.

National Institute of Mental Health (NIMH)
6001 Executive Boulevard, Room 8184, MSC 9663
Bethesda, MD 20892-9663
(301) 443-4513 • Fax: (301) 443-4279
e-mail: nimhinfo@nih.gov
Web site: www.nimh.nih.gov

The National Institute of Mental Health (NIMH) is one of twenty-seven components of the National Institutes of Health (NIH), the federal government's principal biomedical and behavioral research agency. NIH is part of the U.S. Department of Health and Human Services. The NIMH mission is to reduce the burden of mental illness and behavioral disorders through research on the mind, brain, and behavior. It also seeks to achieve better understanding, treatment, and, eventually, prevention of these disabling conditions, which affect millions of Americans.

National Mental Health Information Center
PO Box 42557, Washington, DC 20015
(800) 789-2647 • Fax: (240) 221-4295
Web site: http://mentalhealth.samhsa.gov

The Substance Abuse and Mental Health Services Administration's National Mental Health Information Center provides information about mental health to users of mental health services and their families, the general public, policy makers, providers, and the media via a toll-free telephone number, their Web site, and more than six hundred publications.

National Women's Health Resource Center (NWHRC)
157 Broad Street, Suite 315, Red Bank, NJ 07701
(877) 986-9472 • Fax: (732) 530-3347
e-mail: info@healthywomen.org
Web site: www.healthywomen.org

The not-for-profit National Women's Health Resource Center (NWHRC) is an independent health information source for women. NWHRC develops and distributes up-to-date and objective women's health information based on the latest advances in medical research and practice.

Postpartum Support International (PSI)
(800) 944-4773
Web site: www.postpartum.net

Postpartum Support International is a nonprofit organization whose goat is to increase awareness among public and professional communities about the emotional changes that women experience during pregnancy and postpartum. The organization advocates, educates, and provides support for maternal mental health in every community, worldwide.

Suicide Prevention Action Network USA (SPAN USA)
1025 Vermont Avenue NW, Suite 1066
Washington, DC   20005
(202) 449-3600 • Fax: (202) 449-3601
e-mail: info@spanusa.org
Web site: www.spanusa.org

The Suicide Prevention Action Network USA is a nonprofit organization dedicated to preventing suicide through public education and awareness, community action, and federal, state, and local grassroots advocacy. The organization creates a way for survivors of suicide—those who have lost someone to suicide—to transform their grief into positive action to prevent future tragedies.

For Further Research

Books

Ava T. Albrecht, *100 Questions and Answers About Depression*. Sudbury, MA: Jones and Bartlett, 2006.

Tracy Anglada, *Intense Minds: Through the Eyes of Young People with Bipolar Disorder*. Victoria, BC: Trafford, 2006.

Jean J. Beard and Peggy Gillespie, eds., *Nothing to Hide: Mental Illness in the Family*. New York: The New Press, 2002.

Shoshana S. Bennett, *Beyond the Blues: A Guide to Understanding and Treating Prenatal and Postpartum Depression*. San Jose, CA: Moodswings, 2003.

Nell Casey, ed., *Unholy Ghost: Writers on Depression*. New York: William Morrow, 2001.

J. Raymond DePaulo and Leslie Alan Horvitz, *Understanding Depression: What We Know and What You Can Do About It*. New York: Wiley, 2002.

Jed Diamond, *The Irritable Male Syndrome: Managing the Four Key Causes of Depression and Aggression*. Emmaus, PA: Rodale, 2004.

Maureen Empfield and Nick Bakalar, *Understanding Teenage Depression: A Guide to Diagnosis, Treatment, and Management*. Collingdale, PA: DIANE, 2003.

Dwight L. Evans, *If Your Adolescent Has Depression or Bipolar Disorder: An Essential Resource for Parents*. New York: Oxford University Press, 2005.

Gail Griffith, *Will's Choice: A Suicidal Teen, a Desperate Mother, and a Chronicle of Recovery*. New York: HarperCollins, 2005.

Peter D. Kramer, *Against Depression*. New York: Viking, 2005.

Lisa Machoian, *The Disappearing Girl: Learning the Language of Teenage Depression*. New York: Dutton, 2005.

Shaila Misri, *Pregnancy Blues: What Every Women Needs to Know About Depression During Pregnancy*. New York: Delacorte, 2005.

Kate Scowen, *My Kind of Sad: What It's Like to Be Young and Depressed*. Toronto: Annick, 2006.

Claudia J. Strauss, *Talking to Depression: Simple Ways to Connect When Someone in Your Life Is Depressed*. New York: New American Library, 2004.

Charles L. Whitfield, *The Truth About Depression: Choices in Healing*. Deerfield Beach, FL: Health Communications, 2003.

Periodicals

Mike Fazioli, "Would You Admit to Being Depressed?" *Men's Health*, June 2006, p. 42.

Kate Johnson, "Primary Docs Often Overlook Depressive Symptoms in Elderly." *Clinical Psychiatry News*, May 2006, p. 53.

Barbara Kantrowitz, "'I Never Knew What to Expect'; Depressed Parents Often Leave Their Children a Legacy of Fear and Anxiety." *Newsweek*, February 26, 2007, p. 49.

Eva Marer, "Trouble in Mind; Haunted for Years by Mysterious Aches and Pains, Eva Marer Finally Discovered That the Cause of Her Suffering Was in Her Head." *Vogue*, December 2006, p. 302.

Patrick Perry, "Mike Wallace: Speaking Out on Depression: The Veteran CBS Newsman Helps to Break the Stigma Surrounding a Treatable Disease." *Saturday Evening Post*, September–October 2006, pp. 48–49.

Carol S. Saunders, "Changing Attitudes About Depression." *Patient Care for the Nurse Practitioner*, December 2001, p. 7.

Julie Scelfo, Karen Springen, and Mary Carmichael, "Men and Depression: Facing Darkness." *Newsweek*, February 26, 2007, p. 42.

Dana Slagle, "Why Depression Needs to Be Addressed in the Black Community." *Jet*, October 9, 2006, pp. 48–50.

Penny Zeller, "Dispelling the Top 10 Depression Myths: Understanding Is Half the Battle." *Vibrant Life*, November–December 2006, pp. 10–11.

Index